ALSO BY CHARLEY MARSH

The Destination Death Series in Reading Order

Stalked in Paradise

Masked in Paradise

Frozen in Paradise

Buried in Paradise

Shattered in Paradise

Betrayed in Paradise

Haunted in Paradise

See Charley's website for other books and series in science fiction, mystery, and romance.

https://charleymarshbooks.com/

HAUNTED IN PARADISE

A DESTINATION DEATH MYSTERY

CHARLEY MARSH

TIMBERDOODLE PRESS LLC

CHAPTER ONE

Harriet awoke with a sense of unease. She lay in her king-size bed, caught in that half-awake, half-asleep state, and tried to figure out what was bothering her.

She had her dream job as Public Relations Director for the most highly rated vacation spot on the planet.

Her memories were returning, albeit slower than she'd like.

She had her best friend living next door and she had the man she loved sleeping at her side.

She closed her eyes and let her thoughts roam. She'd been dreaming about her life in Portland, the time right before she came to the island.

It had been a bad time in her life. She had finally come to realize her fiancé was emotionally abusive, that he had systematically cut her off from her friends and especially her closest friend, Solomon Ayers.

On the surface, Bradley Higgins had appeared to be the perfect man. A handsome, charismatic, and respected attorney who owned one of Portland's coveted old mansions that overlooked the Eastern Promenade and Casco Bay, Bradley topped the list of the city's eligible bachelors. When he chose Harriet out of all the women who would love to be his wife, she'd been flattered and honored.

A year later, she had felt trapped, with no one to turn to for help.

Solly had left Portland to fill the position of head gardener for the Island Resort. She wouldn't have even known he was gone if he hadn't left a note for her at the front desk for the ad agency where she worked. The note reflected the diminished state of their friendship: *"In case you still care, I've taken a new job. Leave tonight for the Island Resort. Wish you the best. S."*

She could still vividly recall how she'd felt upon reading Solly's note.

Hollowed out. Gutted. Bereft.

That's when she finally understood what her relationship with Bradley Higgins had cost her.

When the call came a month later informing her that the job of Public Relations Director for the resort was hers if she wanted it, she had jumped on it.

It was one of the smartest decisions she'd ever made.

A snuffling sound came from Harriet's right, drawing her back to the present. A large wet nose pressed against the insect curtains that surrounded the bed.

Harriet suppressed a groan. Despite spending most of Sunday lazing around and napping, her body felt worn out from the traumatic events of the previous few days.

"Belle," she whispered, choking back a cough. Her throat still felt raw and scratchy–she must have inhaled more smoke than she realized from Friday night's fire.

Not wanting to disturb Alex, who was still catching up on missed sleep from trying to solve a recent murder, she tried to push Belle away, but Belle only pressed harder with her nose.

"Are you trying to tell me it's time to get my lazy butt out of bed?"

Belle answered with a soft woof.

"I'm awake." Alex reached over and pulled Harriet in for a snuggle. His large, calloused hand ran up her naked leg and snugged around her waist. "Mmmm, you feel good," he said into her hair.

"So do you." At six-three and solidly built, Alex was one of the few men who didn't make her own five foot eleven feel like a giantess. Amazingly enough, he could make her feel downright dainty, an unusual sensation for a girl who towered over most people, male or female.

"Woof."

"I think Belle really needs to go outside," Harriet said reluctantly. "I'll take her for a run on the beach. Do you want to come?"

"Not this morning. I'm going to shower and head into the office. Tarbell and I are meeting with Payson later about a new security measure for incoming guests. After we nearly lost you last week I think he's finally willing to listen to my ideas. "

Harriet stepped onto her lanai ten minutes later with the giant dog she'd recently adopted and took several deep breaths. The sea was calm, the sun not yet crested over the three mountains that formed the spine of the island. The air felt cool and refreshing and tasted of brine. She performed her pre-run stretches while Belle snuffled around the base of the lanai.

The cottage next door looked empty. Solly's new lover William, the resort's pastry chef, left for the kitchens at an ungodly early hour. Because Solly headed the resort's greenhouses and grounds crew, he was usually up early as well. They used to run together every morning, but not lately.

Another recent change that contributed to Harriet's growing sense of discontent.

"Here we go, Belle." She walked down to where the tide pounded the sand into a solid, cushioned surface and set off at a light jog toward the south end of the island with Belle running easily at her side. As her steps thudded dully on the sand, Harriet let her thoughts wander. Running was her zen, her place of peace and also inspiration. Ideas for new resort ads often came to her while she ran.

Today though, what came was not inspiration, but a recent memory. A guest had asked Harriet a question right before she tried to kill Harriet. The guest's words came back to taunt her: *"How on earth did a lowly advertising drone with no social connections end up as publicity director for the most famous resort on the planet?"*

Harriet had dismissed the question at the time because she had other, more important things to worry about–like staying alive–and then she'd forgotten it. Now she wondered about it.

How did she, a low level ad executive with barely two years experience under her belt–and all of it for small, piddling companies–end up being hired over thousands of more qualified candidates to fill the position of public relation director for the most exclusive resort on the planet?

When she took the job she had had no dealings with, nor had she understood, the resort's clientele: society's upper crust, the privileged, the wealthy movers and shakers of the world. So why was she the chosen one?

It made no sense. She'd been so far down the list of suitable candidates it was laughable to believe anyone would hire her. But because the job had arrived at a critical point in her life, she had never questioned her good fortune until now.

She picked up her speed and ran for several minutes while she pondered the question. When they neared the mangrove swamp that comprised the southern tip of the island the breeze shifted, bringing the faint stink of sulphur mixed with the slight stench of dead flesh–the perfume of the carnivorous plants that made the swamp their home.

A saltwater crocodile grunted and Belle woofed in response

and looked toward Harriet for guidance. The crocs were the apex predator on the island and Harriet steered well clear of them.

"Danger zone, Belle. Time to turn around."

During her early days on the island she would often choose a mangrove tree on the swamp's edge, take off her trainers and sit on an exposed root with her feet in the shallow water, watching small fish and crabs go about their business. She would stare at the horizon and let the magic of the tropical island fill her with peace.

Even though she no longer had time during the day to simply sit and watch the island world, she should feel happy. She had Alex and Solly and new friends and she loved her job—even if people thought she wasn't qualified. She frowned and slowed to a walk.

Belle, ever hopeful despite her huge, lumbering body, chased a small flock of sandpipers down the beach. The white and brown birds easily kept out of the dog's reach and she eventually gave up and returned to Harriet's side.

There was something, something that had been swirling around beneath her conscious thoughts ever since she'd been accused of being unqualified for the position she held. Something that kept banging up against her consciousness.

Harriet moved up the beach to drier sand and sat, folding her long legs beneath her while she thought back. She let her thoughts drift back to the day she had landed the PR job.

She'd been at work, trying to decide whether to stick it out or quit. The job she'd had high hopes for had turned out to be a dead end despite a recent promotion.

When her supervisor—a fifty-something, sweet-tempered, grandmotherly type—plucked Harriet from the pool of the lowest, smallest ad account managers and set her up in her own office, Harriet had felt elated that her career was finally getting off the ground. Her supervisor had finally recognized that Harriet was a step above the other ad managers.

She shook her head over the memory. Her janitor closet-turned-office had smelled of floor cleaner and bathroom deodorizer, and the harsh florescent light overhead made the skin on her hands look sallow. Her desk looked as if it had been through a war, its gray metal sides and top battered and scarred. The drawers grated on their runners with a squeal that set her teeth on edge and stuck when closed all the way.

Still, it had been her first office and she had felt proud to have earned it—until she discovered that she'd been chosen for the promotion because she made the least number of typing mistakes. Her workload increased—not with better ad accounts, but with the typing she was required to do for her co-workers.

Everything that was wrong with her life had come to a head that day.

She remembered the day as if it were yesterday. She hated her job. She no longer had any friends. And she had realized that she disliked and mistrusted her fiancé as well. In short, her life was a mess and it was time to do something about it.

Mind made up, she had grabbed the olive drab canvas pack she still used for a purse and left her office without a word to anyone. It had been cold that day, winter's icy claws still gripping the Maine coast even though the calendar claimed it was spring. People scurried in every direction, no one lingering like they would on a warm spring day. No one paid any attention to her as she headed for a nearby sandwich shop to plan her next move.

She didn't feel the least bit hungry, but she couldn't take a table unless she was a customer and she needed a warm place to sit and think. She ordered fries and hot tea and found a table in the far back corner of the narrow shop, away from the window and prying eyes.

The place smelled of mushroom and nut veggie balls and rich

tomato sauce, yeast bread, garlic, and fresh-brewed coffee. The scarred tables and scuffed wooden floor were testaments to how long Enrico's had been a popular fixture in the city. It had been one of her and Solly's favorite places to go whenever they could scrape together a few extra credits.

For several minutes she did nothing but stare blindly at the table's scarred formica surface. She had felt like a ship caught in that neutral spot between going forward and going backward. Free floating. Adrift. Directionless.

The sensation of being lost had hit her hard. She needed her best friend. She needed someone to help guide her through this sudden upheaval. Someone to help her decide where to go, what to do.

And then her link had buzzed, flashing an unknown number on the screen and her life had changed. She had accepted the job offer, never questioning why the position had been offered to her.

This was why she'd woken with a sense of dread that morning. Her subconscious had been telling her that something was out of whack.

She should never have even been considered for the position. The guest had been right to question her qualifications as she essentially had none to speak of.

But the real reason she shouldn't have been considered was the simple fact that *she had never applied for the position.*

How could she land a job she never applied for?

Harriet stood, brushed the sand from her legs and shorts, and headed for Mermaid Cottage, her beautiful home, one of four, one-bedroom employee cottages set apart from the main resort. She had a large, light and airy office that also sat on the beach. She had the job of her dreams. The life of her dreams.

It was time to find out why.

CHAPTER TWO

The days of the week on the island had a tendency to blend into one another, except for Saturdays. Saturdays were the all-hands-on-deck day, the day the week's guests left and the new guests arrived. Controlled chaos ruled the day, with staff rushing to eradicate all signs of the previous guests and prepare for the incoming.

The scheduling was something that Harriet had been meaning to bring up with the resort's owner. The change-over day pressure on the staff left them frazzled and tetchy, something Payson missed because he steered clear of the main resort on Saturdays. It could all be avoided with one simple change. That made three things she needed to discuss with her boss.

Because she had yet to convince Belle to ride in one of the hydrogen-powered carts the resort provided for transportation, she needed someone to look after the dog while she paid Payson a visit. There was only one person she could ask.

She walked the shell road to the greenhouses with Belle padding at her side. The walk took longer than usual because they had to stop for Belle to sniff everything–plants, dirt, bugs, lizards–Belle's curiosity seemingly knew no bounds.

Harriet had found an online crash course in dog care and knew that Belle's nose was her primary means to learn about her new world, so she understood Belle's compulsion to smell everything. Still, Harriet found her patience wearing thin when the dog stopped for the umpteenth time to check out the base of yet another flowering vine.

It was quickly becoming obvious that some intensive training was going to have to take place soon. She needed to find a co-worker who knew something about dogs and enlist their help.

"Solly!" Harriet called down to the opposite end of the greenhouse where her next-door neighbor and best friend frowned down at a plant. He gave her a distracted half-wave and returned his attention to the plant in front of him.

Harriet loved the greenhouses. There were seven of them, all filled with flowers for the guest's rooms and cottages and the interior public spaces, as well as fresh veggies and some fruits for the kitchens. The air smelled of rich, moist earth mixed with the heady perfume of flowers mixed with green, growing things and spicy herbs.

Stopping beside her friend, Harriet looked at the plant in front of him but couldn't see anything amiss.

"Why the frown?"

"What? Oh. It's a new hybrid."

Solly was a Master Gardener, but one thing that had eluded him was the creation of a new, hybrid plant that he could name after himself and thus ensure his place in the Master Gardener's historic Burbank Archives. With seven state of the art greenhouses at his disposal on the island, he often had dozens of experiments going at the same time.

Harriet gave the plant the stink-eye. The last time her friend had given her one of his hybrids to try it had set her mouth on fire.

"What is it this time? No ghost chili peppers, I hope." Solly had the audacity to grin at the memory of her pain.

"Nope. This one is licorice blended with sweet. I've cross-pollinated Thai basil with stevia."

The stink-eye changed to interest. "Sweet is good."

Solly set down the sharp pruners he'd been using and gave her his full attention. "Shouldn't you be at the office?"

"Yes. But I need to track down Payson first and I can't take Belle. She won't ride in a cart yet and Kidd's Cove is too far away to walk." She waited expectedly.

"Ah. You want to leave the beast with me."

"She's not a beast. She's a sweet girl. Aren't you, Belle?" Belle sat and looked between Harriet and Solly, her tail brushing back and forth across the brick floor.

"Harry, if you're going to keep a dog–and I'm not even sure you can have one on the island–it is a World Wildlife Sanctuary, after all. *If* you can keep her, you're going to have to figure out what to do with her at all times. I'll help now and then, but I'm too busy to keep an eye on Belle on regular basis. What if she digs up my plants?"

She hadn't thought about Belle digging. Did all dogs dig or was it breed related? What she knew about dogs could fill the head of a pin.

"That's why I need to speak to Payson as soon as possible. Please? Just for a little while? I'll come straight back as soon as I finish with Payson, I promise."

"Fine. But you'll owe me." He pinned her with a glare. "And you know I'll collect."

Harriet made a face at him. This was a game they'd played with each other from the first day they'd met as teenaged runaways. "You always collect." She hesitated. "Have you had a chance to ask William who is bothering him?"

Solly scowled. "I tried, but he won't talk about it and I don't want to force the issue. He'll talk when he's ready."

The previous week, Harriet had overheard a link conversation that sounded as though Solly's partner was being threatened, but when she asked him about it William denied it. Recognizing there was nothing they could do unless William asked for their help, she let it go. She had too many things on her mind as it was. Still, it was important for Solly to know she'd be there to help if needed.

"When he does feel ready to talk about it, be sure to tell him that I'll do whatever I can to help."

Solly's gaze softened. "You're a good friend. Give him time. Now scoot. I can only watch Belle for a couple hours so you'd better get going."

"Thanks. I'll be as quick as I can."

She bent down and took Belle's large head between her hands. "Stay here with Solly. Be good for him. We might need him again."

Belle followed her to the door.

"Stay." She opened the door only enough to squeeze through and closed it behind her. Belle stared at her through the glass and barked when she saw Harriet leaving.

Keeping a dog on the island wasn't going to be as simple as she had assumed; there was so much about dog care that she hadn't anticipated. She grabbed a cart from the front of the next greenhouse and headed for Kidd's Cove, where Payson lived.

Traveling the pink crushed shell road that followed the west shore of the island was always pleasant. The ocean sparkled on Harriet's left and the deep, shadowy jungle climbed from the coast to the island's mountains on her right.

A flock of red and blue parrots rose squawking from a tree as she drove by, circled and landed in the same tree once she passed. She wondered if it was the same flock she often saw, or if the birds moved around to different areas. Were they territorial? She knew so little about the island and its natural inhabitants, an oversight she should work to remedy.

As she approached the main resort, more guests appeared on the beach. The resort proper covered a four mile stretch along the island's west shore, with a dozen rustic cabins on the east shore built for when the Wildlife Sanctuary's biologists came to catalog the island's flora and fauna.

Thinking about the east shore cabins reminded her that the WWS prohibited domestic animals on any refuge. It would be foolish for Payson to risk the island's status as a refuge just so she could keep Belle.

What would she do if he told her Belle had to go? She felt bonded to the dog after what they'd been through together. Belle was part of her family now.

She held the cart's wheel tightly, nervous about the conversations she was about to have with the resort owner. Belle was the easy part. Even suggesting the resort change the length of their guest week from its current Saturday through Saturday to a more sane Sunday through Saturday would be easy. Asking why she'd been hired for a position she never applied for would be much, much more difficult.

What if Payson told her he'd made a mistake; that he shouldn't have hired her after all? Would she argue with him? Try to defend herself? She knew she'd been doing a good job, but she hated confrontations and avoided them whenever possible. Now she was about to confront her employer over not one, but three separate issues.

She felt sick inside. Maybe asking Payson why he hired her was a bad idea.

She was approaching the resort's only hotel, a low, two-story affair built from pale cream-colored limestone, when one of the desk clerks waved her down. Glad for the delay, Harriet pulled up and got out of the cart.

"Calida! I'm surprised to see you hanging around the hotel still."

"It seems we have a missing guest," Calida replied in the singsong island lilt Harriet loved. The attractive night desk clerk rolled her bright blue eyes. White teeth flashed in her milk chocolate face.

"I am asked to help look."

"Oh no. Who's missing? How long?" Missing persons on the island usually turned out to be nothing more than misunderstood messages or someone deciding to explore the resort without telling their family or friends. But sometimes it was much more serious and therefore couldn't be ignored.

"A Miss Williams. Her traveling companion say Miss Williams planned to visit the lobby this morning when she got up in order to make reservations for the mystery dinner theatre tonight, but none of the desk clerks spoke to her and she has not returned to their room."

"Maybe Miss Williams decided she needed a little time for herself and took a long walk on the beach." Harriet sincerely hoped that was all there was to it. The last time they had a missing guest it had not turned out well for the guest.

"I too hope that is what happened," Calida agreed. "I told Tarbell I would check the benches in front of the hotel in case the woman grew tired and needed to sit."

"Is Tarbell still inside?" When Calida confirmed that Alex's second-in-command was in the hotel lobby, Harriet abandoned her plan to confront Payson and went in search of him. Missing guest trumped conversation with Payson, she reasoned, knowing full well that she was merely delaying the inevitable.

The hotel's airy, two-story lobby teemed with guests. Potted shrubs and palms mixed with large vases filled with colorful flowers separated numerous sitting areas, most of which were occupied. Several guests stood at the refreshment bar and more waited to speak with the desk clerks. A father caught up with a set of young male twins making for the door at top speed and tucked one under each arm, making them squeal with laughter.

She found Tarbell talking to a couple of very beautiful, very fit gym rats with smooth, tanned muscles and perfect hair. Obviously on their way for a run, they were dressed in matching designer outfits, from their sneakers to the sweatbands on their wrists and brows.

He showed them something on his link and moved to another guest when they shook their heads. Harriet waited until he finished speaking with the guest before interrupting him.

"Tarbell! Calida says you have a missing guest. How can I help?"

The ex-Boston detective's bright green eyes and wide smile were at odds with the sternness of his burly build and military haircut. Tarbell Fox possessed the legendary charm of his Irish ancestors, a charm that came in handy when interviewing suspects and witnesses. Harriet counted him in the small circle of her closest friends even though she'd known him for less than a year.

"Morning, Sunshine. Where's that great beast of yours?"

"With Sol at the greenhouse. I haven't been able to convince Belle yet that riding in a cart will get us around the island faster. Can I see a photo of Miss Williams?"

Turning his link, Tarbell revealed a pretty young woman with long blonde hair. "Patricia Williams, a.k.a. Patty. According to her companion, Patty is not the type to do a Houdini. Nor is she complexy, dicty, or gully low."

"Dicty?" Harriet scowled. "Who on this planet uses a word like dicty? That's not even a word."

"I don't make them up, I just keep them alive."

Tarbell's habit of peppering his speech with old American jazz slang often left Harriet scratching her head in puzzlement. The fact that he was doing it again was a good sign however–it meant his depression over the absence of his new girlfriend had run its course. A depressed Tarbell was a terrible thing.

Although she would never admit it aloud, Harriet had missed the slang talk while he'd been moping. She enjoyed giving him a hard time about it and she suspected he used the most obscure words he could find just to tease her. Words like dicty.

"English, please, Tarbell."

"The allegedly missing woman is neither neurotic, snooty, nor unhappy. She's a warm, generous, genuinely nice person. She would not take off just for the fun of it without informing her companion, a Mrs. Allison Beuckers. Allison also describes Patty as level-headed and responsible."

"How long has she been gone?"

"According to Mrs. Beuckers, Patty planned to speak to the desk clerk early this morning. Mrs. Beuckers slept in, so she doesn't know the exact time that would have been. Apparently Patty is an habitually early riser."

"Does Alex know?"

"He's with the companion now. I'm asking guests if anyone's seen Miss Williams."

"Shoot the photo to my link. I'll walk the beach and show it to anyone I see there."

"Done. Plant you now and dig you later."

Harriet shook her head and headed out.

An hour later, she'd spoken with everyone she encountered on the beach. No one had seen the missing woman. She pulled her link from her pack and called Solly.

"How's Belle doing?"

"She's still sitting by the door waiting for you to walk back in." His eyes narrowed. "You're on the beach. What are you doing on the beach? I thought you were going to talk to Payson and then come back here for your dog."

"I never made it to Payson's. One of the guests is missing. I volunteered to ask the guests on the beach if they'd seen seen her. I'm on my way to you now."

"Ah, geez. If you see Alex or Fox let them know I can help with the search. Or at least I can as soon as you come get your dog."

Harriet flushed with guilt. She knew it wasn't fair to Sol to dump Belle on him. He had a job that kept him straight-out busy and a crew to supervise. He didn't have time to dog sit.

"On my way. Why don't you call Alex and volunteer your help? I'm sure he'll appreciate the extra manpower." Since they'd been on the island, she and Solly had not only helped search for previously missing guests, they had also helped Alex and Tarbell solve several murders.

Too many murders, as far as Harriet was concerned. So many, in fact, that the resort employees had dubbed the island "Destination Death."

When the mainland news feeds had learned about the murders and splashed them everywhere in their irritatingly lurid, sensationalized, and breathless way, Harriet had expected the resort reservations to dry up. Instead, they had exploded. Apparently the jaded wealthy wanted to rub elbows with killers. A few even came to the resort to use it as their killing ground.

Fortunately those guests were in the minority. Most came to have a good time and enjoy all the resort had to offer.

Still, eight dead guests in the seven months since the resort's opening was a terrible track record.

Harriet prayed Miss Patricia Williams would not be number nine.

CHAPTER THREE

"Excuse me."

Harriet jumped and whirled around. A male guest stood several feet behind her. Stepping away from the cart she'd been about to climb into, she studied him. His voice was deep and smooth, the kind of voice she imagined commanded board rooms or self-help seminars.

"How can I help you?"

He looked middle-aged, somewhere in his sixties or so. Silver had recently begun to frost his thick chestnut hair. He was an attractive man: tall, well toned and well dressed. A man who obviously took care of himself.

But his most striking features, the ones that caught and held her attention, were his eyes. Set in a ruggedly handsome face and heavily fringed with dark lashes, his eyes looked like aged pewter. Something about them tugged at her. It wasn't attraction—he was too old for her. But there was something about them that drew her.

They stared back at her until she began to feel uncomfortable.

The man must have sensed her discomfort because he smiled and held out his hand.

"I apologize for staring. You remind me of an old friend and I got lost in memories there for a minute. I didn't mean to make you uncomfortable. I'm Martin O'Claire. I overheard you ask one of the other guests if they'd seen a missing woman."

Harriet smiled and took the proffered hand.

"Harriet Monroe. Yes, one of our guests seems to have wandered off and her friend is concerned."

"Do you have a photo? I've been out and about for several hours. I might have seen her."

Harriet pulled her link from her canvas pack and brought up Miss Williams' photo. Martin took the link from her hand and stared at the photo.

"Pretty girl. I'm fairly certain I saw her in the lobby earlier, getting a cup of coffee." He handed back the link. "I'm afraid I didn't see where she went after that."

Harriet felt a rush of excitement. Someone could verify that Patricia Williams made it to the lobby at least. "That's very helpful, Mr. O'Claire. Can you tell me what time that was?"

"Call me Martin, please. I saw her . . . oh, maybe five-ish?" Mr. O'Claire wagged his head. "Maybe five-thirty. I couldn't sleep, so I thought a walk on the beach would be nice."

"Thank you. I'll let our security director know."

"I think I saw your security director when he arrived at the hotel. Big man wearing a dark blue polo with a resort insignia. Dark hair, broad shoulders? What's his name?"

"Alex Hayes. Is there anything else I can help you with, Mr. O'Claire? I need to be somewhere . . ."

"Call me Martin," he said again. "Please. Mr. O'Claire makes me feel old. I don't need anything at the moment, thank you for asking. I'm sorry I held you up."

Harriet flushed. She hadn't meant to sound rude. "You haven't. It's just that my friend is watching my dog and I needed to pick her up a half hour ago. Enjoy your stay at the resort and don't hesitate to ask the desk clerks if you need anything. They're here to help."

"Thanks, I'll remember that. Good luck locating your missing guest." He turned on his heel and walked away with a loose, swinging gait.

Closing Patty Williams' image on her link, Harriet called Alex and told him about Martin O'Claire sighting the missing woman at the coffee bar earlier that morning.

"That's something, anyway," Alex said. "No one else seems to have noticed her. Are you headed to the office now?"

"I have to pick up Belle first. Then the office." It looked like her talk with Payson would have to be put off a while longer. "Do you want to meet for lunch at the canteen?"

"I doubt that dogs are allowed. I'll bring lunch to you. We can sit on the lanai."

Harriet sighed, climbed into the cart, and headed for the greenhouses. She liked eating at the employee canteen.

Keeping Belle just kept getting more and more complicated.

"You seem awfully quiet. Something on your mind?" Alex plucked a piece of feta from Harriet's Greek salad and crossed his ankles. They sat side by side on her office lanai with their backs against her French doors and watched the guests in the water and on the beach while they ate their lunch.

A light breeze carrying the scent of coconut sunscreen ruffled Harriet's hair. She smoothed it back with a grimace. "I hate to admit this, but I'm completely clueless about what keeping a dog entails. In my defense, I've never had a pet before. I want to keep Belle, but I don't know if I'm smart enough to own a dog. Every time I turn around there's something new to consider."

At the sound of her name, the dog in question thumped her

tail. She lay stretched out beside Harriet, her attention alternating between the guests on the beach and the nearby food.

"Pets are a lot like young children except they never grow up." Alex plucked another chunk of feta from her salad. "You have to know where they are every minute."

"It's not just making sure someone is looking after her at all times–it's also the training. I don't know where to begin or how to do it. I need Belle to start riding in the carts or I won't be able to do my job. If I can't do my job there's no reason for me to stay on the island." She rubbed at the slight ache that was beginning in her temples.

"And I haven't even told Payson yet that I brought a dog back from the mainland with me. What's he going to say? Will the World Wildlife Sanctuary even allow a dog on the island? Ugh. What a mess." She dropped her hands and handed the remains of her salad to Alex before he could snitch more.

"I had to bring her back with me. I couldn't leave her behind after we survived Shonee's attempt to kill us both. I feel . . . I don't know, I guess I feel responsible for her now."

"You do realize that Payson knows everything that goes on here on the island. I'm sure he's well aware that Belle is here and he's waiting for you to tell him yourself. He's the only one who can tell you what the Sanctuary people will say. You need his permission, Harriet. You really shouldn't put it off any longer."

Harriet groaned. "I know. I know. But how am I going to get there? Belle refuses to ride in a cart. And I know that's just an excuse, but it also happens to be true."

"Belle rides in a closed vehicle, doesn't she? Come by the security office and take one of the Hogs. Fox is using one to search the island for Patricia Williams. I can take my bike."

Alex had lovingly restored a Triumph Tiger in his apartment while working as a murder detective in New York City. The only vehicle on the island with a combustion engine, seeing the island from the back of Alex's bike was one of Harriet's favorite things to do. She wondered if that was another thing she would have to give up now that she had a dog.

"Maybe bringing Belle to the island wasn't such a great idea."

"You'll work it out. You just need to get new routines in place."

"And train her."

"And train her," Alex agreed. "But first you need to ask Payson if you can keep her. Take the Hog."

"Okay. I'll head to Kidd's Cove after lunch. I take it the search for Miss Williams has turned serious?"

"Yep. She hasn't been seen since the sighting at the refreshment bar early this morning."

Harriet knew that the lack of security cameras on the island troubled Alex. He had lobbied hard for them to be installed after the first murder, but Payson had refused, citing the guests' need for privacy.

Security cameras were everywhere on the mainland–a person could hardly take a step without being caught on a camera. They were a fact of modern life and ignored by most citizens. Or at least ignored by the law-abiding. She assumed that criminals hated them.

Alex planted a kiss on Harriet's temple and set her empty salad container on her lap. "You'll work it out." He took Harriet's hand and laced his fingers with her own.

"I need to get going. Let me know how the talk with Payson goes. I'll let Mary know you're taking the Hog." He kissed her fingers and released her hand, stepped off the lanai, and disappeared around the corner of the building.

Harriet sat for several more minutes, steeling herself for the upcoming meeting with Payson. She didn't know why she hadn't mentioned the other thing she needed to discuss with Payson–

the fact that Payson had hired her for a job she never should have been considered for.

"Crap. Okay, Belle. We might as well get this over with."

While the Hogs were the workhorses for the security department, the resort carts were used for day-to-day getting around by guests and employees alike. Like she'd told Alex, getting Belle to ride in the carts was essential if she was going to do her job.

To her relief, Belle jumped right into the Hog. The heavy-duty, hydrogen powered all terrain vehicles served many purposes. Faster than the guest carts, the resort's two Hogs carried equipment and people into remote areas and also served as the island's ambulances. Harriet had never driven one, but it only took a minute to figure out the power, brakes, and steering.

Although she had loaded Belle into the rear seat, the dog immediately squeezed into the front to sit beside Harriet. She rode with her head stuck out the passenger window, her long ears flapping in the breeze. Harriet didn't know if it was safe for her to ride like that, but Belle looked so happy she didn't have the heart to raise the window.

Payson lived in the farthest cottage on Kidd's Cove. Four crescent-shaped coves named after infamous pirates offered guest cottages ranging in size from two to four bedrooms, ideal for visitors who didn't want to stay in the hotel. Kidd's was the farthest from the main resort area.

Harriet had just taken the left-hand fork that followed the island's coastline when her link buzzed. She pulled to the side of the road to answer it.

"Alex, what's up?"

"We have another woman reported missing."

"What!" Despite the warm day, Harriet shivered. "What's going on?"

"I don't know, but it can't be good," Alex said, his voice grim. "Can you meet Fox at the amusement park and help him search?

Afternoon's are relatively busy and two sets of eyes will make the search go faster. I'm headed off now to search the circus grounds."

The circus performers were on their summer tour of the continent. Guests could freely wander the circus grounds, but there wasn't much to see other than empty tents and booths. The trapeze and hi-wire equipment had been dismantled and stored away, removing any temptation from those foolish enough to test their skills.

Feeling guilty to have a legitimate excuse to put off her conversation with Payson, Harriet tried not to sound too eager. "Sure. I'm not far from there. I just turned onto the left fork. Tell Tarbell I'll meet him in two minutes at the gate." She backed the Hog around and turned onto the shell road's right-hand fork.

The amusement park was one of the guests' favorite attractions. Sugar white beaches and five star hotels and dining could be found around the globe, but the amusement park was unique to the resort.

The park's manager, Braxton Holliday, had spent several years tracking down rides and games of skill from long-dead amusement parks around the world and restoring them back to their former glory. Six months of that time alone was spent searching for the animals from the last known wooden carousel–hand carved animals several hundred years old that were sold off to collectors from all corners of the globe.

The newly restored carousel and the roller coaster–a wild and crazy ride that hurtled above and through the other park rides– were the only surviving examples of once popular amusements. The park was colorful, noisy, and a huge draw for children and adults alike.

Harriet pulled onto the sandy parking pad near the amusement park entry gate and parked next to the security department's other Hog. Tarbell leaned against the front fender, working his link.

"Thanks for lending a hand," he said, standing straight. "I just shot you a photo of the second missing woman. Her name is Azzi DeBerry. We have no idea when she disappeared. Her roommate, Miss Krystina–that's Krystina with a K and a Y–Miss Krystina Griffin, last saw her at the rooftop restaurant around one a.m., give or take, where they were both partying with a couple gentlemen whose names she cannot recall."

"Why did it take Miss Griffin so long to report her friend missing?" Harriet opened the passenger door for Belle.

"Here." Tarbell pulled a length of rope from the back of his Hog and fashioned a slip knot. Sliding the loop over Belle's neck, he handed the other end of the rope to Harriet. "It's crude, but it will work until you get a proper collar and leash."

Taking the rope, Harriet thanked him.

"As for why it took so long for Krystina-with-a-K-and-a-Y to report her friend missing, Miss Griffin slept in this morning and didn't knock on Azzi's bedroom door when she got up because she assumed Azzi was also sleeping late. When lunch came and went she decided it was time to roust her friend, but there was no sign of Azzi."

"Could she tell if Azzi slept in her bed?"

"Very astute question. She thinks so, but couldn't say with absolute certainty. She left the restaurant before her friend and didn't hear her friend come in."

"And the gentlemen? What did they have to say?"

"Brothers. Gary and Daniel Whitfield from Omaha, Nebraska. Claim Azzi left the rooftop restaurant about fifteen minutes after her friend. They stayed another hour." He held up his hand. "Before you ask, confirmed by the bartender on duty and the bar droid. The brothers were apparently celebrating a big real estate deal they'd just closed and were quite gregarious."

Harriet pulled up the photos of the two missing women on her link. Although they looked nothing alike, they shared one common feature.

"They're both blonde."

"Yeah. Alex and I noticed. Let's get going. I have a bad feeling about this."

Harriet kept her link out with the two photos, took a solid grip on Belle's leash, and followed Tarbell through the gate.

CHAPTER FOUR

Harriet was hit with a melange of smells as soon as she and Tarbell walked through the amusement park gate. The scent of grilling cajun fish tacos mixed with coconut sunscreen and sugary, spun cotton candy. Children shouted and laughed and raced through the guests, calling to one another and their parents. The clack-clack of the roller coaster underscored the music from the carousel. The park was a raucous and happy place, the guests smiling and relaxed.

It was hard for Harriet to believe that beneath all the gaiety lay the ugly possibility that something bad had happened to two of their female guests.

"We'll stick together, work opposite sides of the path," Tarbell said. "Less chance of missing anyone that way." They headed toward the right, taking the winding path that would lead them around the park and back to the gate. Because the resort limited the number of people on the island, none of the resort's amenities ever became crowded; a fact that made questioning the guests easier.

Despite this, it was slow going. They stopped everyone they came to and showed the photos of Azzi and Patricia, asking if they'd seen the missing women. Some people remembered seeing them earlier in the week; several had seen Azzi with her friend Krystina in the hotel's rooftop restaurant the previous night. No one had seen either woman that day.

As they made their way through the park, Belle walked sedately by Harriet's side. She tried to pull away once, when a nearby child dropped a piece of food. Harriet quietly reprimanded the dog and tugged on the lead. She felt quite pleased when Belle returned to her side with a heavy sigh and a soulful look that made Harriet want to laugh.

At the rear of the amusement park, water slides had been built into a natural waterfall. It was a favorite spot for the groups of orphans Harriet brought to the island for one week every month; consequently she ended up spending a fair amount of time there, often joining them on the slides.

Mostly she enjoyed sitting in the cool shade on one of the wooden benches that surrounded the natural pool at the bottom of the slides and watching "her" kids enjoy themselves. The orphans were the best part of her job. In her mind they balanced the scales, making the island available to the poor as well as to the wealthy.

She made a point to video the orphans enjoying everything the resort had to offer, gifting them with a new link pre-loaded with her personal link number and a copy of the video as a reminder of their time on the island.

She had also set up a corporate-funded education account to help them once they left the island. As an orphan who had come from the streets, she knew first hand how difficult it could be to get a foothold on the ladder that lifted a person above the poverty level and she was determined to do everything she could to give other orphans a chance for a better life. What would happen to them if she had to leave her job?

"Earth to Harry. You with me?"

"Sorry. I was thinking about my orphans."

Harriet had been surprised and pleased at how the resort's employees donated their free time to help with her kids. Because of them and the generosity of the guests and mainland businesses, the program was well-funded and reaching a point where she could expand its reach.

A mother shouted for a little boy to watch out as he stood at the bottom of a slide, then waded in to pluck him out of the way just as another child shot out of the tube.

Harriet considered the two missing women. It was unlikely that Patricia and Azzi had disappeared themselves. She pictured their bodies tossed into the thick jungle where they'd never be found, or tossed into the sea where the crabs and fish would feast upon their soft parts. She shuddered.

"Cancel those thoughts," she said aloud. God, her brain was like a butterfly flitting all over the place. She really needed to catch up on her sleep, but at the moment she needed to focus on the task at hand.

"Cancel what?" Tarbell frowned at her.

"Nothing. I'm imagining things I don't want to imagine." Harriet led Belle to one side of the wide, shallow pool to see if she wanted a drink, but Belle surprised her by wading into the water and lying down on the sandy bottom with a blissful groan.

"Leave her be," Tarbell advised, when Harriet tried to coax Belle from the water. "She isn't hurting anything and I imagine the cool water feels good to her. It's going to take a while for her to acclimatize to the island's temperatures."

Harriet gave her friend a considering look. "You sound as if you know something about dogs."

"Some. My folks had dogs when I was growing up. They have pretty basic needs: food, a safe place to sleep, ground rules, and love. They'll put up with a lot of abuse because they're genetically pre-disposed to bond with the hand that feeds and cares for them early on." He nodded toward Belle who was now snapping at the water in a strange form of play.

"Despite being an adult, Belle has already bonded with you, Harry. You'll do fine together. Teach her to sit, stay, and heel. That's all you really need."

"Will you help me? I'm feeling a bit overwhelmed at the moment."

Tarbell flashed a grin that made him look like a big, bad-assed teddy bear. "You bet. Soon as we find these women. Why don't you start showing their photos to everyone down here; I'm going up to question the monitors at the top of the slide."

He headed toward a discreet set of stone steps that led to the top of the waterfall and swiftly climbed them. Belle watched from the water while Harriet spoke with the guests occupying the benches around the natural pool. No one had seen either woman that day. Tarbell rejoined her and they coaxed Belle from the water.

"Oh, jeez. Belle!" Harriet laughed and held up her hands to protect her face from the water flying off Belle's coat as the big dog shook. She picked up the wet rope lead and they continued down the path, stopping everyone they met and showing them Azzi's and Patricia's pictures.

By the time they reached the gate, she no longer felt like laughing. There had been no sightings of Azzi since she had visited the rooftop restaurant with her friend, and no one had seen Patricia since she was sighted at the hotel lobby refreshment bar early that morning.

"It's like they vanished into thin air," Harriet complained as she loaded Belle into the Hog.

"As opposed to someone vanishing into thick air? What is thin air, anyway?" Tarbell asked.

"Ha-ha. This is no joking matter. We've lost two guests, Tarbell. Two! You know this can't be good. I don't think I can deal with this right now."

On the preceding Thursday she had undergone an intense and sometimes painful procedure on the mainland to eliminate the blocks that prevented her from accessing any memories before the age of eight. She had always believed her aunt's story that her parents had died in an accident, but she was tormented by the fact that she had no memories of them.

After the procedure she was shaken by the discovery that her parents had belonged to a New Age cult called the Bliss and, according to news reports, the entire cult had committed suicide. Her parents had chosen to leave her an orphan.

When she visited what was left of the cult's home on Friday–hoping to jar loose some memories–a bitter old woman tried to kill her and she spent the night trapped in the woods. When she returned to the island the following day someone else had tried to kill her.

All in the space of three days. Meanwhile, a new group of guests meant she had to plunge back into work. Despite sleeping away most of Sunday, she felt exhausted and frazzled and in need of a vacation from her life. Which she recognized as a bit of irony since she lived on the most coveted vacation spot on the planet.

Harriet mentioned none of this to Tarbell. He was a good friend but only Alex and Solly and Payson knew about her past.

"Now where should we look?" She scratched Belle's head through the open window.

"Let me call Alex and see what he has to say." Tarbell placed the call and angled his link so they could both see Alex's face.

"No luck at the amusement park, Alex. Did you learn anything?"

"No. I drove up to the north end of the island in case one of the women decided to head up there even though it isn't part of the main resort. Nothing. I also checked the circus grounds and searched the tents. Again, nothing."

"What next?" Despite an overwhelming desire to return to Mermaid cottage and crawl into her bed, Harriet knew they had to keep looking for the two women.

"I'm on my way back to the hotel to search the women's room again in case I missed something. Tarbell, I think we need to search all the boats at the marina. Can you handle that?"

"On it, boss."

"What about me? How can I help?"

"What about your meeting with Payson?"

"It will have to wait. Finding the two women is more important."

Alex didn't argue. "Come to the hotel and help me search their rooms. You might notice something I'd miss."

"I'm on my way."

Tarbell cut the call and slid the link into his pocket with a grim expression.

"It doesn't look good, does it? Where can they be?" Harriet rubbed her fist over the cold knot growing in her belly. "Where can they be?" she repeated.

"We'll find them. It is an island after all. Unless they're in the belly of a croc they'll show up sooner or later."

Harriet glared at him, horrified. "Not funny. Don't even joke about that. I keep imagining them lying hurt or dead somewhere. Otherwise someone would've seen them today."

"Yeah, I'm not too happy that no one has seen them. I've got some boats to search. In a while, crocodile." He winced. "Sorry about that. Habit."

Harriet pulled up to the hotel several minutes later, remembered to pocket the Hog's key, and skirted the edge of the lobby with Belle on her makeshift lead. Despite her effort to keep Belle out of sight, they were noticed.

"Mama, look at the giant dog! Can I ride it?"

The mother shushed the little girl and led her from the lobby with a worried side glance at Belle. Harriet picked up her pace and turned right, down the corridor leading to Patricia's room. All of the hotel's guest rooms in that wing were off to her right, facing the beach. The opposite, windowless wall of the corridor faced the jungle and was decorated with paintings by island artists, alternating with retro-style wall lamps in handblown, pale aqua glass.

Colorful bouquets of fresh flowers set on small tables between the suite doors perfumed the corridor air.

An older woman with purple hair piled on top her head in an elaborate do answered Harriet's knock.

"Hi. I'm Harriet Monroe. I'm supposed to meet Alex Hayes here. The resort's security director?" she added, when the woman merely blinked at her.

"Just a moment." The woman closed the door, leaving Harriet and Belle standing in the corridor. It opened a moment later. Alex had the purple-haired woman by the elbow, leading her into the corridor.

"Why don't you go up to the rooftop restaurant and enjoy a cold cocktail while Harriet and I search your friend's room, Mrs. Beuckers. We won't be long. I'll send someone to get you as soon as we're finished."

The woman escaped Alex's hold and turned to go back into the room.

"I need to watch and make sure you don't touch anything you shouldn't. Patty would want me to watch over her things."

Harriet slipped inside the door with Belle, effectively blocking the way.

"Please, Mrs. Beuckers," she said quietly. "Let us do our job.

You can do a full inventory when we're finished, but I promise you, we aren't interested in your friend's things except if they can help us figure out where she might have gone off to. We'll treat them with care."

She saw tears in Mrs. Beucker's eyes and knew the woman was afraid for her friend and fighting to hold herself together. Wrapping her arm around her shoulders, Harriet whispered in her ear. "We'll do whatever it takes to find her, I promise."

Mrs. Beuckers nodded and drew herself up. "I think I'll sit out front and wait for you."

Alex shot Harriet a grateful look. "I'll personally come find you when we're finished, Mrs. Beuckers," he said.

"Allison. You may both call me Allison. After all, you'll be pawing through my knickers, I imagine. We might as well be on a first name basis." With that she trotted off down the corridor.

Harriet smiled and shook her head. "Poor dear. She's afraid for Patricia and I can't blame her." They walked into the two-bedroom suite. Belle plopped down on the rug in front of the settee. Harriet decided that was as good a place as any for her and left her there.

It took them fifteen minutes to search Patricia's room thoroughly and Allison's room lightly. They found nothing that shed any light on where Patricia might have gone.

Harriet made sure everything was back as they'd found it, then returned to Alex. He was staring out the sitting room window, thoughtful.

"Patricia's been kidnapped, hasn't she?" she said, moving to stand beside him. "Someone grabbed her this morning and took her somewhere." He turned to her, his expression troubled.

"It's the most likely scenario, much as I hate to think it," he agreed. "And I'm afraid Azzi DeBerry has been taken as well. The question now is, where are they being kept? If they're still alive, that is."

"What about the east side of the island?" Harriet asked. "Has anyone searched the cabins there yet?"

"Not yet."

Twelve rustic cabins stood on the island's east shore, accommodations for the scientists and biologists who visited the island to survey the flora, fauna, and geology of the island for the World Wildlife Sanctuary. Harriet had visited the cabins several months earlier to search for another missing woman–a search that hadn't ended well. She quickly shut down that line of thought.

"Let's search DeBerry's room again while we're here." Alex led the way further down the corridor, stopping at the next to last room.

Searching Azzi's room yielded as much as Patricia's had–nothing.

"I'm going to tell Mrs. Beuckers she can return to her room, then I'm going to head to the marina and give Fox a hand searching the boats. It's getting late. Why don't you take Belle back to the cottage and feed her?"

Harriet placed a kiss on his jaw. "Call me when you finish." She wanted to keep looking, but Belle needed her dinner. Harriet knew she should also eat, but her stomach felt too knotted for food. She drove the Hog back to Mermaid Cottage, fed Belle, and poured herself a glass of white wine.

She couldn't stop thinking about the missing women. That led her to the victims who had their lives taken from them while vacationing on the island. And back to the missing women. Where were they? Were they alive? Or did they have two more victims?

"Harry. Harry!" Harriet had been standing at the open lanai door, lost in thought. Startled to find Solly standing in front of her, she sloshed the glass of wine she had poured and promptly forgotten. Solly grabbed the glass and set it on her counter.

"From your expression I'm guessing the two women are still missing."

Harriet closed her eyes to hold back her tears and shook her head. She felt Solly's arms pull her in for a hug and leaned against her friend.

"I don't know if I can work here any longer," she croaked.

CHAPTER FIVE

Solly held Harriet's shoulders and pushed her far enough away to see her face. "What do you mean you can't work here any longer?" Despite her distress, she could feel his hands trembling slightly as they held her.

"Why on earth not?" He sounded angry, but he always sounded angry when something unexpected upset him. She tried to order her thoughts, which were admittedly a jumble, and explain the way she felt.

"Everything is such a mess. I know the women are probably dead and I can't take any more death. The island–or at least the resort, because there are predators on the island, like the crocodiles–"

"Harry. Slow down. You're talking nonsense. First of all, you don't know that the women are dead so stop that talk. And second, you're completely worn out and not thinking straight. You've been through a hellish lot in a very short period of time and you haven't had any time to process what happened to you.

"For chrissake, someone tried to kill you–twice in as many days. Cut yourself some slack. Your emotions are raw, and understandably so. That's all this is. You'll feel more yourself after a few good nights' sleep."

Harriet grabbed her friend's shirt with both hands. "It's not just feeling overtired, although you're right, I am," she conceded. "My parents were murdered, Solly, along with forty-six other adults and twenty-nine children. Twenty-nine children were murdered and I should have been number thirty. One crazy-assed woman took all those lives. I don't know how to process that." Tears pooled in her eyes.

"And here on the island–a place that should be a safe, happy place–bad people keep showing up and cutting innocent lives short. There's too much evil here. I don't want to live where bad things keep happening anymore." Despite her effort to hold back the tears, they began to track down her cheeks.

'Ah, sweetie." Solly pulled her close and held her. "Nirvana doesn't exist. There's evil everywhere."

Harriet turned her head sideways so she wouldn't get his shirt all wet and saw William standing on the lanai looking uncomfortable.

Embarrassed to be seen in such a messed up state, she pulled away, rubbing the tears from her face with her fists.

"William. Hi. I'm afraid you caught me having a bit of a melt-down." Blinking away the tears that still threatened, she managed half a smile.

The resort's pastry chef had only recently moved in with Solly next door, an adjustment she was still finding difficult to get used to. Although the pastry chef hadn't said anything she could pinpoint, she felt she had to watch how she behaved around him. She couldn't shake the feeling he was watching her and judging.

She hoped that as she grew to know him better that the underlying tension she felt would ease, but so far William had resisted any of the attempts she had made to talk about some-thing other than pastry.

"I don't feel like cooking so Will and I were going to grab dinner at the canteen," Solly said. "I came over to see if you wanted to join us. I assume Alex is busy and thought you might like some company."

Although Harriet appreciated her friend's thoughtfulness, she felt too too raw to have to watch her words and actions around Will. She patted Solly's arm and moved to the opposite side of her kitchen island.

"Not tonight, but thanks for thinking of me." She took a long guzzle of her wine, then realized William was watching her and set it down with a sharp crack on the island's granite surface. Solly gave her a worried look.

"Sorry. I think you're right, Sol. I do need to catch up on my sleep. I'll hit the mattress early tonight. Thanks for the dinner invite. Maybe next time."

Solly was reluctant to leave her. Ten minutes of meaningless conversation later, Harriet closed and locked the door after him and William with a sigh of relief. Her friend was right; her nerves felt raw and exposed–lying on the surface where they could be scraped by the slightest thing.

After giving Solly and William enough time to head to the canteen, she topped off her wine glass and headed back out to the lanai with Belle following close at her side. She was beginning to see the attraction of keeping a dog. They didn't ask questions and expect answers. They were just there–undemanding company.

She needed to sit undisturbed, drink her wine, and let the sound of the waves and the sea breeze work their magic on her. The sun would be setting in a couple hours, at which time she could go to bed and put this bloody awful day behind her.

She walked down the steps and stood beside the lanai for several minutes, twisting her bare feet in the warm sand to relieve some of her tension before settling onto her favorite cushioned lounger. She let her head fall back and stared at the purple-bottomed clouds.

She felt as if she'd been on a non-stop roller coaster from the moment she had walked into Dr. Bainbridge's office four days earlier. Since that day, she'd been carried along by events she had no control over. Unable to stop and catch her breath. So much had been going on that she hadn't had a moment to simply sit and see if any memories would rise to the surface.

"Don't try to force them," the doctor had told her. "Let them come naturally. You'll see something, or hear something–even smell something–and it will trigger a memory. They'll come. Be patient with yourself."

The doctor had known what he was talking about, she realized. She had remembered her friend Danny when she saw his grave marker. And remembered picking apples with her father when she saw the orchard on the side of the hill.

Seeing Margaret Blackstone's cabin she had recalled sitting on the porch and playing with the rag doll her mother had made for her. She wondered what had happened to that doll. She supposed it had burned along with everything else when the cult's longhouses were torched by Margaret after the mass murder.

Yes, the memories were coming back, but not fast enough to suit her. What games did she play as a child? How did her parents behave around one another? Were they openly affectionate? Did her mother read to her? Her father? Who were their friends?

Movement on the beach caught Harriet's eye. She recognized the fitness couple she had seen earlier that day in the hotel lobby. As they drew closer she realized they were dressed once again in matching outfits. A small laugh burbled out of her. Whoever said it took all types to make the world go round had been onto something. She waited for them to pass before lifting her wine glass in a toast.

The breeze shifted so she could no longer feel it on her face. Small waves met the shore in a frothy jumble and receded with a soft, rhythmic, mesmerizing whoosh. The tension she'd been carrying in her shoulders began to ease. Belle sat at her side, alert for the small flocks of shorebirds that darted along the water's edge.

A lone figure appeared on the beach, walking toward the south end of the island. Something about the way the man moved looked familiar. As he drew closer, she recognized Martin O'Claire.

It was too late to stand and move inside without being seen. With luck, he wouldn't notice her. Or if he did, she hoped he would respect her privacy. The last thing she wanted to do was to make small talk with a stranger.

Unfortunately, luck was not with her.

"Miss Monroe!" Martin O'Claire turned up the beach and stood at the edge of her lanai. "I thought I recognized you. Is this where you live?"

"Yes." It was rude not to say more, but Harriet couldn't muster the energy to be polite.

"Beautiful spot. Nice cottage. One of the perks of the job, eh? Have you located the missing women yet?"

"Not to my knowledge." Belle watched O'Claire, but she didn't seem duly alarmed. Harriet relaxed slightly. "Are you enjoying your stay?"

"Definitely. The island is beautiful, although I'm not sure I'd want to live here year round. I'm a four season man myself."

"I know what you mean. I haven't been here long enough to know if I'll miss winter or not. Where are you from, Mr. O'Claire?"

"Martin, please. All over, really. I go wherever my work takes me. I'm a preacher."

"Ah." With his deep voice, rugged attractive looks, and arresting, silver gray eyes, she imagined he was popular with his parishioners.

"What about you? Where are you from?"

"I grew up on the coast of Maine. A long way from a tropical paradise."

"Mind if I sit?" He indicated the step.

Harriet hesitated. She didn't ever want to invite a stranger onto her lanai, but especially after Patricia and Azzi's disappearances. Before she could think of an excuse, Martin held up his large hands.

"That's all right. I understand. You don't know me and it's good to be cautious. I should be going anyway. I'm meeting friends for dinner but I wanted to stretch my legs while it was still light out. It's been nice seeing you again, Miss Monroe. Have a good evening, and I hope you locate your missing guests soon." He headed down to the water and turned back up the beach toward the resort.

"Well, that was badly done of me." Harriet felt an uncomfortable mix of relief that O'Claire was gone and embarrassment over her rude behavior. She watched the preacher's long legs eat up the ground until she lost him in a group of people.

Suddenly, she felt painfully aware of how isolated and vulnerable she was. Before O'Claire's visit she had been reveling in the solitude. Now she felt . . . afraid. Afraid of what? No one was going to attack her with Belle at her side.

She really should have gone to dinner with Solly and William.

"I am such a mess. Come on, Belle. Let's go for a walk. Maybe it will help clear my head." She set down her wine glass and headed in the opposite direction from the preacher, grateful to have the massive dog's company.

While she walked, she tried to empty her mind and concentrate on the usually soothing sound of the waves, to no avail. It had to be a combination of lack of sleep and the events of the previous few days that were making her feel weak and vulnerable and jumpy. Out of control.

Her nerves felt like a rubber band that was stretched to its breaking point. What would it feel like to snap?

If she didn't do something soon she might find out.

Patricia Williams tried to open her eyes but something was holding them closed. When she tried to remove it, she realized her hands were tied. As were her legs. She wanted to call out but there was something in her mouth.

She was bound and gagged and blindfolded.

She stilled, terrified that someone was with her and would realize she was awake. What could they want with her?

She fought the tears that threatened. If she cried, her nose would clog and she would suffocate.

She was in a world of trouble.

Straining to listen, she heard only her own racing heart thudding in her ears. The scent of sandalwood wafted toward her.

Someone was with her. Captor or another victim like herself?

She felt a prick followed by a warm rush of bliss. Her situation no longer mattered. Nothing mattered but the sensation of floating above the world and all its troubles.

CHAPTER SIX

Harriet woke with Belle's cold damp nose in her neck. "How did you get in my bed?"

There was no sign of Alex. She grabbed her link from the bedside table and saw she had three missed calls.

The first was from Alex, saying he would sleep at his apartment over the security office as he would be working late.

The second call was from Alex, wondering where she was and if she was all right. He sounded worried.

The third call was also from Alex, sounding much more relaxed. "Never mind," he said. "I called Solly and he told me you were probably still in bed. Call me when you get up."

Harriet rubbed Belle's ears while she waited for Alex to pick up.

"Sorry I worried you," she said. "I went to bed early and never heard the link. Any sign of Patricia or Azzi?"

"None. I'm about to head over the mountains to the east side to check on the cabins there."

"Why don't I meet you at your office?" Harriet suggested. "Belle and I can help you search."

Alex hesitated.

"Taking the Hog over the mountain will be safer than your bike," she pressed. "And I want to help. I won't be able to focus on work until both women are found."

"All right. I'd love your company."

Harriet showered and dressed in record time. She called in an order for breakfast and several sandwiches to go while she drove to the offices, swinging by the canteen to pick them up before she met up with Alex.

"Belle, out." Alex moved Belle to the rear seat and took her place in the front. He looked tired and hadn't bothered to shave, although she could see he had showered and put on clean clothes. Added to his crooked nose and the scar through his right eyebrow, his beard's dark shadow made him look even more dangerous than usual.

It was no wonder he'd had a high solve rate when working as a NYC murder detective. The criminals probably took one look at his face and knew he'd never quit so confessed.

"You want me to drive?"

"Why not? Can you handle it?"

Harriet pictured the rough and muddy jungle road. "I think so. You can always take over if I get stuck."

"It'll be good practice. Just don't drive too fast and we'll be fine."

Picking her way through potholes and puddles and over and around obstacles took all of Harriet's concentration. Alex remained quiet, occasionally guiding her to the left or right of a large puddle. Her hands began to tire from gripping the wheel so tightly and a sharp pain had blossomed between her shoulder blades.

"This is harder than I expected," she mumbled.

"Would you like me to take over?" Alex sat slumped in the corner of the seat. Several times she'd glanced over and saw that his eyes were closed. He had to be exhausted.

Her body leaped at the offer, but she shook her head. "No. You're right–it's good practice. Other than the shell road, I've never driven anywhere that wasn't smooth and paved before, and the resort road is plenty smooth. This is kind of fun."

As soon as she said it, she realized she really was enjoying herself. Driving under rough conditions took constant mental focus. For the first time ever, she felt as if she was truly driving a vehicle and not just steering something that mostly drove itself.

Plus there was the added bonus that there was no room for the thoughts that had been plaguing her.

The road over the mountain was little more than a muddy path; a dark, narrow tunnel through the jungle. Vines hung down and slapped loudly against the roof of the Hog. Limbs and leaves scraped against the vehicle's side, and mud splattered and sprayed from beneath the tires. Twice she had to stop and wait for Alex to cut away a fallen tree.

"I think we need to do more regular maintenance on this road," he said after clearing the second tree. Mud covered his boots and chinos up to his knees and spattered his forearms.

"Or we could let the jungle take it back and get to the cabins by boat," Harriet pointed out. She frowned at him. "Why *didn't* we take a boat? It's faster and far easier."

"Two reasons. One, if the missing women wandered onto this road we wouldn't know unless we drove it." He looked out the window.

Harriet waited. When she couldn't stand it any longer, she let out an exasperated sigh.

"And reason number two?" Alex turned his head to look at her. Harriet's breath left her body at the expression in his eyes.

"I needed some uninterrupted time with you. It's been crazy since you got back. I know this isn't a great time. I know it's only been five days since you started getting back your memories. I know you need to figure out life with Belle. To top it off, we're missing two female guests–I know all that. But the thing is . . ." He stopped, took a deep breath.

"The thing is, I could have lost you when that madwoman tried to poison you. When I heard that, Harriet, I froze inside. Knowing how close I came to losing you–I can't stop thinking about it. I pictured taking you for a ride on the Tiger to the north headland and doing this there at sunset, but that's unlikely now and I can't wait any longer."

Confused, Harriet shook her head but it didn't help clear things up. "You want to take me for a ride on the Tiger?"

Alex groaned. "I'm doing a piss poor job of this. I know this isn't the most romantic spot or time, but I feel as if I've been waiting forever. I want to get married, Harriet. I want to make it official. I love you and I want to make a family with you. Here on the island. Or on the mainland if you prefer–we'll live wherever you want. I don't care where we end up, as long as I have you at my side."

During his speech, Alex had clasped one of her hands between his large ones. He lifted it to his lips and kissed her fingers, one by one, sending delicious little shivers down Harriet's spine.

"Please say yes. But you should know–" He gently squeezed her hand and released it. "–you should know that once you say yes I'll want to have the wedding as soon as possible. Six months is too long to wait. Six weeks would be too long. Six days would make me happy."

When Harriet watched him without speaking, some of his confidence began to ooze away. She saw uncertainty come into his eyes.

"Say something."

"Are you finished?"

"Yes." He held himself very still, his breath shallow, as if by moving he might alter her answer somehow.

"Okay, then." She took a deep breath. She hadn't been

expecting a marriage proposal, even though Alex had made it clear that he loved her.

"I love you, too, but you already know that." She hesitated. Hated the withdrawal she saw in his eyes but it couldn't be helped.

"I love you with all my heart, Alex, but I can't say yes–yet. There's something I need to clear up first."

She felt deeply touched by the way Alex's heartfelt proposal had been delivered and was filled with love for the man sitting beside her covered in mud. The proposal might not be Alex's idea of romantic, but to Harriet it had been perfect, a moment she would cherish and relive for the remainder of her days. She hated that she couldn't give him a yes.

"Can you talk to me about it?"

"It's-it has to do with Payson and could affect my future."

Alex watched her, his gaze steady, waiting.

Embarrassment wouldn't let her share her newly realized self-doubt. Would his feelings toward her change when Alex discovered she was woefully under qualified for the position she held?

"I'll tell you everything after I've spoken to Payson."

"Harriet–"

"Please."

He watched her for a long moment, trying to read her.

"Whatever time you need. I'm not going anywhere. You can't shake me, Harriet–unless you decide you don't love me. All I ask is that you be honest with me."

His tone changed, became brusque as he turned to look out the windshield. "All right, let's see if our missing guests are hiding on the east side of the island."

Harriet breathed a heavy sigh of relief when the Hog exited the jungle. The side opposite the resort had been left undeveloped except for the basic necessities. There was no pretty pink shell road for Harriet to follow, only rough, gray rock that dropped off to a wide, crescent-shaped cove. The sun's rays reflected off the water, nearly blinding her after the deep shadows of the jungle.

Twelve small cabins lay stretched along the curve of the shallow bay.

"Mark told me that these cabins weren't in the original resort plans," Harriet said, as she pulled in behind the northernmost building.

Mark Fortner, the chief financial officer for Wade Enterprises, had become a close and cherished friend after they spent a night together in one of the cabins.

Nothing had happened that night, due entirely to the fact that Mark had refused to take advantage of Harriet's inebriated state; a fact that caused her more than a little embarrassment when she let herself remember how badly she'd behaved.

"He said the World Wildlife Sanctuary required access to the island before they'd give it sanctuary designation. Payson didn't want the biologists and scientists taking up guest space so he had these cabins built."

Belle immediately began to sniff the ground after they exited the Hog. She headed for the nearest cabin with Harriet and Alex following.

"Can't say that I blame Payson," Alex said, as they crossed the bare rock that lay behind the cabins. Fox and I took a boat over here a few months ago. There was a small group here taking water samples and one of them had gotten lost. We searched the cabins—which were a muddy mess. Their lost biologist showed up just as we were about to head into the jungle to search. He'd forgotten his GPS and got himself turned around. Fortunately he was sampling a stream and was smart enough to follow it back to the coast."

It only took them a half hour to search the dozen empty

cabins. They were not only unoccupied, they looked as if no one had been in them since Alex and Fox's last visit.

The simple, two-bedroom cabins were bare-bones, with four twin beds, a galley kitchen with a two-burner gas cooktop, a bathroom with shower only, and four chairs and a large table in the living area.

When they finished their search, Harriet retrieved the food she'd brought and they carried it down to the float at the end of the central dock—one of three that provided boat access and docking for the cabins.

"This side of the island feels so different from the west side." Harriet handed Alex a napkin and a fork for his cold pasta and shrimp salad. They sat back to back and leaned against each other for support. Harriet lifted her face to the sun.

"It feels wilder," she continued. "Harsher. It reminds me more of the Maine coast."

"It is wilder. The east side of the island gets the full force of storms coming off the Atlantic. The west side gets the storms too, but not as fierce because the mountains block a lot of their energy. That's why the resort is built on the lee side of the island. Plus, the ocean beats against this shore, which is probably why it reminds you of Maine. "

They concentrated on their food and finished their lunch in a companionable silence. Harriet fed Belle from a box of leftovers the kitchen had provided. She made a mental note to ask Eleanor Clarke about Belle's diet. The resort's resident doctor had raised dogs on the mainland and would be a good resource for Belle's health care and general needs.

"Now what?" she asked. "Have we searched everywhere you think the women might be?"

"Not quite. I'll drive us back."

They packed up the empty containers and headed back to the

Hog. Harriet strapped into the passenger seat, then released the strap and leaned over to plant a kiss on Alex's jaw.

"What was that for?"

"I love you. I hope you'll ask me to marry you again–and soon."

"Nope." A glint appeared in his eyes.

Harriet's heart stuttered. Had she missed her one chance? He had said he'd wait; now he was changing his mind?

"But you said–"

"When you're ready, you'll have to ask me. I'm not setting myself up for rejection again."

CHAPTER SEVEN

Once they made it back over the mountain, Alex made arrangements to meet up with Tarbell Fox at the security office. Few resort guests had reason to visit the compact, two story stone building tucked unobtrusively behind the kitchens, but those that did were surprised to find it looked nothing like a mainland police station.

When Harriet followed Alex inside, they were greeted by Alex's office droid Mary, who stood at attention behind the waist-high counter in the wide, shallow lobby. In contrast to the lobby's friendly appearance, the stern-featured droid wore a permanent frown on her square, pug-nosed face, a frown that Harriet couldn't help but take personally. No matter how many times she stopped by the security office, Mary always frowned at her and always insisted on a scan to verify Harriet's identity.

Leading Belle to the refreshment bar in the back corner of the comfortable lobby, Harriet filled a cup with water for her. Belle slurped noisily from the cup, getting as much water on the gleaming wood floor as she did in her mouth. From the corner of her eye, Harriet caught Mary staring at her. Obviously she would clean up after Belle; she didn't need the droid's disapproval to make her do the right thing.

She consoled herself with the thought that Mary hadn't insisted on an identity scan–probably because she'd arrived with Alex.

"Anything to report, Mary?" Alex asked.

"No, sir. No calls. No visitors."

"Good. We're expecting Fox. We'll wait for him in Conference Room Two." Alex appreciated the two no-nonsense droids provided by the resort to aid him. Because droids required downtime to recharge and perform system checks and the security office needed to be manned around the clock, he switched them out on an every other day basis. Identical in looks and temperament, he had named both droids Mary.

"Yes, Sir. I will inform Mr. Fox where to find you when he arrives."

"Thank you, Mary." Alex held the door to the left wing for Harriet. "You'll be more comfortable in here, I imagine," he said. His eyes twinkled. He knew his droids made her uncomfortable–unlike her own office droid, a handsome, dapper Englishman named Jeeves who wore a welcoming smile and greeted Harriet with friendly banter whenever he saw her.

The security office's two conference rooms were as comfortable as the lobby. No scarred walls, hard plastic seats, or offensive odors for the resort's wealthy guests. They were treated like royalty even when they were being questioned.

Conference Room Two held a half-dozen thick-cushioned chairs covered in a bright peach and white floral pattern arranged around a low, polished steel topped table. A drinks trolley set against the right wall held a variety of refreshments. Unlike standard interrogation rooms, this one had a large window that looked out onto the jungle and several colorful landscapes of the island painted by local artists hanging on the walls.

Harriet poured herself a glass of fresh pressed lemonade and drank half of it down before she took a seat next to Alex. The cold, tart-sweet drink felt good on her smoke-damaged throat. She hoped the fire Friday night hadn't caused permanent damage to her vocal chords. Her voice was husky enough as it was.

She was a natural contralto like her mother. A memory of singing with her mother while they weeded their garden allotment made her blink. Before she could tell Alex, Tarbell came through the door and the opportunity passed.

"Fox." Alex indicated the chair across from him. "Any sign of either woman?"

"Nothing. No one saw or heard anything, Alex. It's like the earth swallowed them up. Poof. Hello, La Bella." He bent down to rub Belle's ears before he sat.

"I wasn't holding out much hope. Still–" Alex sighed.

"Yeah. Still. You can't help but hope."

"There was no sign of them on the east side either. Waste of time to go there, but we had to check."

"Absolutely. So where does that leave us?"

Alex drummed his fingers on the table. "I hate to say this, but we need to search all of the guest rooms at the hotel, and then everyone's cottage. If we were only missing one guest, I'd say she got lost. But with two missing–I'm afraid that someone, or some-ones, has taken those women and squirreled them away. Or worse."

Tarbell grimaced. "I have to agree. Those women didn't both wander off on their own."

"If the room and cottage search doesn't turn them up, we'll have to round up the droids and employees and search the roadsides."

Harriet's breath caught. If they were searching the jungle

along the edges of the resort roads that would mean they'd given up any hope of finding the women alive. They would be looking for dead bodies.

"Have you done a background check on the guests, the men in particular?" Tarbell asked. "We could be dealing with a serial kidnapper."

"No, and I need to do that." Alex rubbed the spot between his eyes with one finger. "But I can't be in two places at once."

"Harry can help me search the hotel rooms," Tarbell suggested. "It should go fairly quick with both of us."

"I don't want Harriet to search alone. Especially when we don't know what we're dealing with." No one said aloud that Harriet was in the right age bracket and hair color to fit the profile of the missing women, although they were all thinking it.

"We'll stay together, I promise." Tarbell gave Alex a pointed look. "That will free you up to run brief checks on our guests, see if anyone deserves a closer look."

Alex still looked unconvinced. Harriet placed her hand on his arm.

"Let me help Tarbell, Alex. You need to run those background checks. I'll keep Belle with me. You know she won't let anyone hurt me. Solly said to call if you needed more help. He can partner with me after Tarbell and I finish with the hotel and we can help you search the pirate cove cottages. We'll be able to cover them a lot faster with four of us searching."

"It makes the most sense," Alex admitted, "but I still don't like it." He brooded for a long minute. Harriet kept quiet, knowing that he was still feeling raw from nearly losing her twice in as many days.

"All right. I'll call Solly. Come back here when you're finished. We'll decide who should search which cottages then. With any luck I'll have a better idea of who our guests are."

Alex headed through the steel security doors that led to his office. Harriet and Belle accompanied Tarbell to the hotel in the Hog. When they parked, she put her hand on his arm to stop him from leaving the vehicle.

"If someone did kidnap those women, they'd have to be pretty clever to do it without anyone noticing anything."

"Agreed." Tarbell relaxed back into the seat and waited for Harriet to make her point. She liked that about him; he was always patient with her–and not just her. She'd seen him exhibit patience with all women, even the ones who'd try the patience of a saint. Saint Fox. The thought almost made her smile.

She took a breath and searched for the right words.

"If someone is that clever, then it's unlikely anything will show up on a background check, right? What I mean is, if they've done this before–kidnapped women–they'll have gotten away with it."

Tarbell squeezed Harriet's hand. "That's true, but the checks still need to be done. You have to understand that sometimes it's what's not there that is as–or even more–important than what does show up. If something feels hinky about one of our guests, Alex will sense it."

Feeling slightly better, Harriet nodded and exited the Hog. She put Tarbell's makeshift lead on Belle and they headed into the lobby. She hated the idea of invading the guests' privacy, but consoled herself with the knowledge that it was far more important to find Patricia and Azzi. No decent person would protest a search once they understood that lives were at stake.

And the ones who still complained? They weren't worth worrying about.

She waited near the wall just past the front desk and watched the guests while Tarbell stopped to get a master key. Fitness Couple were returning from a swim, towels slung around their necks in an identical manner. Their sameness weirded her out. How boring it would be to live with someone who mirrored you.

Was there any spark in their relationship? She didn't see how there could be.

The couple stopped at the refreshment counter for tubes of water before heading up the wide staircase to the second level, their steps matching exactly.

"All set. Let's start up and work our way down." Tarbell led the way up the stairs and turned toward the left hand corridor. Harriet caught a glimpse of Fitness Couple entering the room at the far end of the right hall.

"I just saw the couple go in the room at the end of the other hall. If we hurry we can catch them before they hit the shower." They hustled down to the end of the corridor and Tarbell rapped his knuckles sharply on the door.

Fitness Guy answered the door clad only in a short towel wrapped low on his hips. Embarrassed, Harriet averted her eyes.

"We need to search your rooms for two missing guests," Tarbell told him. "It will only take a few minutes and we won't disturb your personal items. Could I have your name and can you tell me who else is here, please?" He pushed past Fitness Guy as he spoke the last bit.

Fitness Guy sputtered. "What's the meaning of this? You have no right-"

"Perhaps I wasn't clear." Tarbell stared down the guest. "Two female guests are missing. We have the hotel owner's permission to search the premises. Now, what is your name and is anyone here with you?" Despite his mild tone, Harriet knew Tarbell had taken a disliking to Fitness Guy.

Two red splotches appeared on the guest's cheeks. "Rodney Lynch," he answered stiffly.

"Rod, honey, what's taking you so long?" Fitness Girl appeared in one of the bedroom doorways wearing a thong and nothing else. Harriet couldn't help but notice her breasts–high and round and they didn't jiggle even a tiny bit when she moved.

Fitness Girl gave Harriet a cold look eye before turning a wide smile on Tarbell.

"Put something on," he told her, and turned toward the opposite bedroom. "Harriet." Grateful for an excuse to leave the room, Harriet followed him into the second bedroom.

"Check the bathroom. I'll look under the bed and in the closet. Then you can wait in the hall to make sure no one tries to sneak out after if you don't want to see Rod Honey and his companion again." His green eyes sparkled with merriment.

Harriet pressed her lips together to stifle a giggle. "I hope that's the worst I'm forced to see." She disappeared into the bathroom. "The bathroom is clear. I'll search the decks and sitting room closet while you do the other bedroom."

They were in and out of Fitness Couple's suite in less than five minutes.

Tarbell shook his head. "Beats me why people work so hard to look like plastic dolls." He knocked on the next door. When no one answered he used the master key to let them in.

Most of the rooms were empty and the search went quickly. The few people who were in expressed concern over the missing women and were only too happy to let Harriet and Tarbell conduct a quick search. Several offered their help if an island-wide search became necessary. Tarbell thanked them and made a note of their names.

"That's it then." They entered the lobby after searching the last of the rooms. Harriet waited off to the side again while Tarbell returned the master key to the desk clerk.

"What about the infirmary and the other spaces that are off limits to the guests?" Harriet asked, when he returned to her side.

"I asked hotel personnel to check them while we did the guest rooms. All clear."

Harriet ran her gaze over the guests occupying the seating areas in the lobby but no one caught her eye. They sat quietly reading or chatting amicably, with drinks and snacks from the refreshment bar.

"People will be getting ready for dinner soon," Tarbell said. "Let's get back to the office."

"Harry!" Solly leaped up from the bench where he'd been waiting in front of the security building and hurried over to meet them at the Hog. Belle gave him a good sniff before sitting at Harriet's side, a move that surprised and delighted her. Maybe training wouldn't be as difficult as she imagined.

Solly searched their faces. "Alex told me you were searching the hotel. I take it the search came up empty."

"We found diddly-squat," Tarbell answered. "Are you here to help us search the cottages?"

"Yeah. Alex said to wait for him. He should be out any minute. He only had a few more names to run when we spoke." He'd barely finished the sentence when Alex came striding out the door with his motorcycle helmet in one hand.

"Nothing?"

"Nada. Any luck with the searches?"

"No. Everyone looks innocent. Whoever our kidnapper is, he's either escaped detection in the past or he has done an excellent job covering up his past."

"Or they have," Tarbell pointed out. "We could have two people working together." Everyone stood silent while they digested this. A team would have an easier time abducting the women. It could explain why no one saw anything.

"What about Martin O'Claire?" Harriet asked. She pictured the attractive man with the arresting pewter eyes. "Is he really a preacher?"

"Yes, but apparently an unusual one. He has no set congregation, but travels where he's invited. He's also quite wealthy. I looked at him a little harder since he was the last person to admit seeing Patricia Williams and I didn't find anything that made my antennae quiver. He also owns a security company that specializes in protecting private homes. Has locations in all the major US cities. "

Harriet's shoulders slumped. She had hoped Alex's background checks would find the kidnapper and put a swift end to the ugly business.

"What's the plan?" Solly moved to stand beside Harriet. "Do you want us to team up or should we separate?"

"I want you to stick with Harriet, please. I'd prefer that she go to her office and wait for us to conduct the search, but she insists on helping.

"Who's going where?" Tarbell asked.

"I'll take the Triumph and search Blackbeard's. Fox, you take Black Bart's. Meet me at Morgan's Cove when you finish and we'll do it together."

"That leaves Kidd's for me and Harry," Solly said.

Payson lived on Kidd's Cove. Harriet knew Alex had assigned them Kidd's for just that reason. It was not only the least likely place to find the missing women, but she would also have to see Payson. She really didn't want to risk running into him, not when she'd been avoiding him for the last few days.

She pursed her lips and narrowed her eyes at Alex, ready to argue, but he had turned away to put on his helmet, his mind already focused on the next task. The Triumph roared to life and Alex took off. Tarbell followed a minute later in the Hog.

"Let's go. I'll drive." Solly climbed into the remaining Hog's driver's seat. Harriet loaded Belle into the rear seat and climbed into the front. She didn't mind if Solly drove. She'd had enough driving that morning and was starting to feel worn out. She needed another week to recover from the past few days, but there would be no rest until the women—or their bodies—were found.

Azzi DeBerry didn't realize something was wrong right away. When she tried to open her eyes and couldn't, she thought they were crusted shut. She'd been pretty wasted when she finally went to bed and hadn't bothered to remove her eye make-up. A big no-no, she knew. Her mother had taught her better than that. But then her mother had been gone for several years now.

Those two guys from Nebraska had been a lot of fun to party with. She rather fancied the younger one—what was his name? Gary. Gary and Daniel something. Brothers. Maybe she'd try to bump into Gary later, see if she could finagle a dinner date.

She tried to wipe at her eyes, but discovered she couldn't move her hands. She kicked out, testing her legs, but they wouldn't move either.

A small kernel of worry blossomed in her chest. She didn't always make the smartest of choices, especially when she had indulged in too much to drink. Was this a sex game carried too far?

It was then that she came awake enough to understand that she was blindfolded, gagged, and trussed up. She couldn't see, couldn't cry out, couldn't move.

Panic set in and she struggled against her restraints.

She felt a prick in her neck and warm comfort spread through her body. She let it take her, because warm comfort beat panicked fear any day.

CHAPTER EIGHT

Solly guided the Hog down the narrow shell road that led to the last of the four developed coves. Named after infamous pirates who were reputed to have visited the island, each cove had a different personality, as did each cottage. Spaced well apart, planted for privacy, and ranging in size from one-bedroom—similar to Harriet's Mermaid Cottage—up to the largest four-bedroom, each of the single story cottages had been designed to blend in with the landscape.

Harriet's breath always caught when the jungle-shouldered road ended abruptly and a wide, white sand beach edged with turquoise water took its place. Of the four coves, Kidd's was her favorite, and in her mind the most beautiful.

The soft breeze off the water hit Harriet as soon as she exited the Hog. The cove was protected from the stronger ocean breezes by its shape—a nearly closed Cee with a narrow gap leading to the open ocean. Fortunately the soft breeze was enough to keep any irritating insects away.

She stood gazing at the view for a long moment and wished she was one of the guests with nothing on her mind beyond relaxing and enjoying what the resort had to offer, instead of searching for two people she increasingly feared were dead.

"Ready?" Solly came around the front of the Hog to join her. Harriet grabbed her canvas bag and slipped the lead over Belle's neck. She had debated leaving the dog in the vehicle, but then thought that would be rather cowardly. She was here, she might as well introduce Belle to Payson. She stifled a groan at the difficult conversation she knew awaited her.

"You okay?" Solly frowned at her. "You still look exhausted, if you don't mind me saying. Alex shouldn't have let you come."

Harriet stiffened and glared at her friend. "Don't you start. Alex had no choice in the matter. I'll catch up on my rest once our missing guests are found. Come on, Belle." She stalked off toward the first cottage, struggling to compose her face into a smile before she rapped on the door.

Each cottage was unique in construction with its own decorating style and a name plaque over the door, another way in which the Island Resort stood out from other resorts with their cookie-cutter rooms and cabins. The cottages were comfortably furnished with plenty of cushy chairs for sitting, roomy beds dressed in luxury bedding, and fully stocked kitchens for snacking–or if a guest was so inclined–cooking.

All but two of the cottages were empty–a relief for Harriet–and took no time to search. She preferred the empty cottages. She felt like an intruder, an invader of privacy, entering a cottage when the renters were away; and so conducted her searches as quickly as possible. To her dismay, Solly was the opposite. He made up sarcastic and often humorous stories about the lives of the absentee guests.

The people in the remaining two cottages were only too happy to cooperate with the search and offered their assistance if more bodies were needed to comb the island. Harriet took their names and link numbers and thanked them.

"That just leaves Payson," Solly said, when they locked up the last cottage.

"I need to speak with Payson anyway so I'll do it."

Solly's eyebrows raised in question.

"I need to tell him about Belle," Harriet answered. She didn't care to examine the reason why she didn't want to tell her closest friend the truth, but there it was. She didn't want to tell Solly that she didn't deserve her job. "Would you mind taking a cart back and leaving me the Hog?"

"You don't want me with you as back-up?" Solly asked in surprise.

Harriet did want him with her as back-up, but not if she was going to ask Payson why he had hired her. That had the potential to be an uncomfortable and possibly humiliating conversation. It would be better if there were no witnesses.

"It's no big deal. Payson will either tell me I can keep Belle or banish her from the island. Either way, I'll be fine. You can probably meet up with Tarbell and Alex at Morgan's Cove and catch a ride back with Tarbell."

The look Solly gave her told Harriet he wasn't completely buying her explanation. Trying to pull the wool over the eyes of the person who knew her as well as she knew herself was no mean feat. She opted for honesty and a little begging instead.

"Please, Sol. I have to do this on my own. I'll talk to you later, okay?"

Solly pulled her in for a hug. "Whatever you want. You know I'm always there for you, right?"

Harriet nodded, too moved to trust herself to speak. The day she'd met Solly had been the luckiest day of her life. She shook off the desire to cry. Apparently Solly was right–if her emotions were still so close to the surface, then she must need more rest.

"All right, then. Talk to you later." He released her and headed back toward a cart sitting outside one of the empty cottages.

Harriet squared her shoulders and turned to face Payson's cottage. Set apart and older than the other cottages, it occupied what she thought of as the right elbow of the cove.

"Come on, Belle. It's time you met my boss." Belle set off as if she knew exactly where they were headed. While they walked, Harriet went over the arguments and questions that had been plaguing her.

When she took the job, she had known less than nothing about the resort's clientele–they could have been aliens from another planet for all the contact she'd had with the wealthy–despite her betrothal to Bradley Higgins. Brad had been a big fish in a very small pond; most of the resort's clientele were whales in the planet's biggest ponds.

She knew her name couldn't have been on the list of potential candidates. She should never have been even a tiny blip on Payson's radar screen.

She needed answers–and only Payson could give her them.

Feeling a bit more determined, she knocked on Payson's door frame and called his name. The inner door was open and she peered through the screen door. Belle sat and wagged, her tail sweeping back and forth on the lanai.

Payson came out of the spare bedroom, the one she knew was filled with the computers and communication equipment that enabled him to run his vast business empire from the island.

He was dressed in his favored loose linen pants and top, his feet bare, his white hair tied back with a simple leather strip. Pausing for half a beat, he took in Harriet's shadowed eyes and the dog at her side.

"Harry. I'm delighted to see you." He held the door open. "Let me get you something cold to drink. How about a glass of wine?"

"Water would be better, thank you. And maybe a bowl of water for Belle?" She entered the cottage and followed Payson back to the kitchen. Unlike her cottage, which was built shotgun-style with all the rooms in a row so they faced the ocean, Payson's cottage was built with the kitchen behind the living room, facing the jungle.

Payson's collection of finely carved wooden masks, some of them over a thousand years old, adorned the living room walls. She tried and failed to ignore their sternly disapproving expressions. Why had she never noticed that none of the faces looked happy?

Although she knew in her head she was being fanciful, the masks' expressions felt personally aimed at her. She walked faster, anxious to escape their censure.

When she entered the kitchen, Payson had already pulled a deep blue stoneware pitcher from the chiller and was pouring her a glass of water. He handed it to her before filling a bowl for Belle and placing it on the floor.

"I planned to come see you later," he said, replacing the pitcher in the chiller. "You've saved me a trip."

Harriet heard the mild accusation in his tone. Her legs felt weak and wobbly. She plopped onto a stool at the blue granite island and took a careful sip of the drink, the liquid sloshing slightly because her hand was shaking.

She couldn't do this. She hated confrontations. What did it matter how she got the job? She loved it and wasn't planning to leave. She should just let sleeping dogs lie.

With her next breath she knew she had to know.

Apparently her inner argument was displayed on her face because Payson frowned. "What is it?"

Out with it, Harriet. Be brave. She traced the condensation on her glass so she wouldn't have to look at him.

"Why did you hire me, Payson? You didn't even know me. It makes no sense."

He took the seat across from her.

"You didn't even know me," she repeated.

"You'd be wrong about that," Payson answered calmly. "I've kept tabs on you ever since you left Apple Valley at the age of eight."

Confused, Harriet looked up. Payson's pale blue eyes regarded her steadily.

"Apple Valley? What does Apple Valley have to do with hiring me? How did you even know about Apple Valley?" When he didn't answer she began to feel a spark of anger.

"I don't understand. Were you a member of the Blissed cult?" Something that resembled relief passed over Payson's face.

"You've remembered. Good. Ed called after you left his office Thursday. He couldn't say if his efforts were successful or not. When Rod told me you'd asked him to fly you to the valley, I was hopeful."

"You've been pushing me to reclaim my memories for months now." Harriet frowned. "I don't understand why they matter to you."

Payson had been supportive of her regaining her memories from the beginning. He had brought Dr. Bainbridge to the island not long after her arrival and introduced her to the psychiatrist. He had taken her to Bainbridge's office on the mainland more than once, seeking to help her regain the first eight years of her life.

She narrowed her eyes. Before she left for the mainland this last time, Payson had told her Dr. Bainbridge was leaving for Vienna right away and would be unavailable to help her for at least a year, something she now knew to be an outright lie. Why? Why were her memories important to Payson?

"Payson," she pressed. "You wanted me to remember. Why?"

Instead of answering her, Payson left the room. He returned with a framed holo that he handed to Harriet, then moved to stand by the back door and stared out at the jungle.

Harriet turned over the holo. A much younger Payson looked

back at her. He had his arm around a young girl with black curly hair. There was no mistaking the adoration in the girl's expression as she looked up at him. She recognized Payson's cottage in the background.

"My half-sister." His voice sounded strained. "Taken here on the island, as you can see. She loved this place. Her mother, Celeste, took off when she was a baby. My father didn't want any reminders of Celeste, so he gave my sister up for adoption. I tracked her down and paid off the adoptive parents, then applied for legal guardianship. The most rewarding thing I've ever done. She was more like my daughter than a sister."

Harriet winced at the pain and wistfulness in Payson's voice.

"She was a beautiful child. You must love her very much."

"Yes." His voice tightened. "I did. She's dead now."

CHAPTER NINE

Harriet set down the holo of the pretty young girl and Payson.

"She's gone? I'm so sorry for your loss, Payson."

The words felt inadequate, but they were all she had to offer. So many losses. Her parents. Payson's half-sister. Alex's sister. She supposed anyone who loved suffered a loss sooner or later. Did the loss haunt them forever? Or did they eventually find a way to move past it?

Although the sun was still shining bright and steady outside the cottage, she felt as if a shadow had moved into Payson's kitchen.

Payson went on as if she hadn't spoken. "She was a good person. Generous to a fault and determined to make a difference in the world." The ghost of a smile crossed his face. "She used to lecture me on doing good with my money."

He lost the smile and his voice hardened. "Then one day she attended a rally for sustainable farming and she met a man named Mayo Sinclair."

He turned his head to look fully at Harriet. Dread pooled low in her belly. She knew what was coming and she didn't want to hear it. She would have jumped up and run from the cottage if not for the fact that she wasn't sure her legs would support her. Payson must have seen what she felt on her face because he nodded once, his gaze locked on hers.

"My sister joined the Blissed cult and moved to Apple Valley. I tried several times to get her away from him, but she insisted they were in love and refused to listen to my arguments."

He turned back to the door, but Harriet knew he wasn't seeing the jungle–he was looking into the past.

"And then it was too late." A bitter note crept into his voice. "She gave up her life for a man who cared nothing for his followers. A man who led them all to their deaths."

At least here Harriet could offer something that might help Payson's pain. "Your sister didn't commit suicide."

Payson's head jerked around. She wanted to shrink back from the mix of pain and anger she saw in his eyes, but forced herself to sit still.

"How can you say that? You lost your parents the same day. It was the top news story for months and still gets resurrected whenever the media needs something sensational."

"The media, the police, the medical examiners–they all got it wrong," Harriet said. "None of the cult members expected to die that day. They were poisoned–murdered–by a jealous, vindictive woman who wanted to hurt Mayo by destroying his followers and his reputation."

Crossing the room to the island, Payson spread his hands on the smooth granite top and leaned toward her. "Tell me what you remember," he demanded.

Harriet took a deep swallow of her water. The cold, bright liquid felt good on her sore, tight throat.

"I only remember small bits from my life with the cult so far," she warned him. "I went to Apple Valley to see if it would help me remember my parents. There's a stone monument there that mentions betrayal." She closed her eyes and brought up the image of the words.

"*The thing that is worse than death is betrayal,*" she quoted. "*I could conceive death, but I could not conceive betrayal.*" She opened her eyes. "I looked it up. It's quote from–"

"Malcom X. I'm familiar with it." Payson waited.

"I met the woman who put up the monument while I was at my parents' graves. She called herself Shonee, but her birth name was Margaret Blackstone. She was a renowned chemist who fell in love with Mayo Sinclair and helped bankroll his cult. She purchased the land where the Blissed lived."

Harriet told Payson everything she knew. She told him about her visit to the cult's home in Apple Valley and how Margaret Blackstone, now an old woman, had waited for her to return all these years; and when she did, then tried to kill her. She told him how Margaret had created the street drug named Blitz and made it for Sinclair to sell to help support the cult.

She told him how members of the cult had disapproved of the drugs, and how they'd grown disillusioned with Sinclair's promiscuous lifestyle and begun to leave.

Finally she told him how a beautiful young woman named Penelope took Margaret's place in Mayo Sinclair's affections. In retaliation, Margaret poisoned the cult members.

When Harriet finished talking, her voice had become a rasp. She slumped on the stool, drained.

Payson sat silent for several long minutes, absorbing the truth about the sister he had loved and raised as his own child.

"You have proof of this?" he eventually asked.

"I saved Margaret's four most recent diaries from the fire. They cover the years she was with Mayo Sinclair right up to the night she tried to poison me."

She returned to the living room where she'd left her pack and brought the diaries back to the kitchen and she set them on the island. In the bright light of day she could see mold growing in the cracks that criss-crossed the leather covers.

Hesitating briefly, she pushed them toward Payson. He looked at them with an expression of disgust before pulling them toward him.

"Before I read these, I have something else to show you." He led the way through the back door. "We need to take a short hike."

On the far side of his parking pad, Payson picked up a narrow, hidden trail and plunged into the jungle with Harriet and Belle following behind.

While the path was surprisingly clear under her feet, the same couldn't be said for the growth above. She pushed aside flowered vines and large, smooth leaves that slapped against her arms and legs, willing her tired body to keep up with Payson.

The trail quickly veered to the left and followed the water, ending abruptly in a small clearing. Three white marble head-stones rose from a carpet of sweet smelling, small blue flowers. Payson stopped in front of the marker to the right and motioned Harriet forward.

"Here lies Penelope Swanson Wade," she read softly. "Taken from us far too soon. The planet weeps with those who loved her." The image of a weeping earth with angel wings was carved into the stone above the words.

Penelope—was this *the* Penelope, the woman Margaret Black-stone hated so much?

"Oh, Payson. Your sister was the woman who stole Mayo Sinclair's affections from Margaret?" Harriet's eyes burned. She wanted to weep with the planet. She laid a hand on Payson's arm and squeezed gently.

"I am so, so sorry."

His pale blue eyes were bright with unshed tears when he looked at her. "I'm thankful to finally learn the truth. All these years I thought I'd failed her somehow, otherwise why would she take her own life?" He took a deep breath and blinked several times, making a visible effort to get control of himself.

"Penny knew your mother and father and shared their long-house when she first joined the cult. She would write me about the things they did together. That's how I knew about you. She often related funny stories about you and your friends. And some not so funny, like the time your friend Danny hit you with a bat and broke your nose."

Harriet rubbed the bump on her nose. "So that's how it happened. It's always bugged me, not knowing why I have this bump."

Payson pulled her hand through his arm and led her to the other two grave markers. Harriet gasped and looked at him.

"How–?"

"They were Penelope's dearest friends. Your parents mattered a great deal to her. When no one showed up to claim their bodies, I had them brought here to bury with my sister."

"But why would Margaret erect grave markers for them in Apple Valley?"

"I can't answer that. At least not until I've read her diaries." He released her hand. "Take all the time you need. I'll wait in the cottage."

Harriet didn't hear him leave. Just offshore, a sleek seal head broke the surface of the smooth water and stared at her, as if curious to see her reaction to the discovery of her parents' real final resting place.

She sank to her knees between their graves and cried for all the heartache one evil woman had caused. When Belle whined and pushed against her, Harriet wrapped her arms around Belle's neck and buried her face in her fur and continued to cry until she had no more tears.

CHAPTER TEN

The sun had dropped toward the edge of the ocean by the time Harriet felt ready to leave her parents' graves and stars were already beginning to sparkle in the deepening sky.

Perhaps it was the release of tears, or merely the fact that she was running on empty, but she felt as hollowed out and fragile as an empty, dried husk.

At the same time she felt strangely at peace, a first in her life. The peace probably wouldn't last, but it would return. She had answers now; enough to build on. She followed the path back to Payson's cottage and knocked on his back door.

"Thank you," she said, her voice a raspy whisper. "Thank you for not leaving my parents in Apple Valley and thank you for tending their graves."

Payson stood back from the door and gestured her inside. "Let's eat. Then we'll talk some more."

Two plain white plates and matching bowls sat on opposite sides of the blue granite island. He filled the bowls with hot, creamy soup, lifted grilled sandwiches from a fry pan, and set them on the plates.

"Sit. Eat."

She didn't need a second invitation. Her stomach felt hollow. "Tomato soup! And grilled cheese sandwiches? My favorite."

"This was my sister's favorite, too."

They ate in a comfortable silence. The recent strain that had developed between them after Harriet had learned of Payson's secret identity had disappeared. After clearing their dishes, they returned to their seats and Harriet waited for him to speak. She still had questions that needed answers.

"I knew you had survived," Payson began. "I had an arrangement with the local chief of police to let me know if anything unusual or illegal happened with the cult. He called me as soon as Margaret Blackstone reported the mass suicide. I flew in immediately and had you whisked out of sight before the news hounds arrived, then informed your aunt that you were alive."

Harriet could only imagine how the media must have salivated over the story and the ensuing frenzy, competing with one another to come up with an angle no other news feed had. If they had known of her survival and tracked her whereabouts, she wouldn't have known a moment's peace.

"Thank you for that."

"You're welcome, but at the time it was entirely selfish. I wanted to know what happened that day and you were the only person left alive who could tell me. Mayo Sinclair had disappeared, and I didn't know about Margaret Blackstone's connection to the cult. Everyone believed her story about the mass suicide and I was no exception."

"Is that why you hired me for a job I wasn't qualified for?"

A smile came into Payson's intelligent blue eyes for the first time that day.

"Who says you aren't qualified? You've done a smashing job, better than I ever could have hoped for–from anyone. Certainly better than any other candidate who applied would have done." He took her hand and squeezed it gently.

"You are excellent at what you do, Harry, and I couldn't be happier with my choice." His expression grew serious.

"I was shocked to learn your aunt had wiped your memories. Doubly shocked at the cruel way she did it. I hired private detectives to keep tabs on you, especially after you ran away from your aunt's home."

He hesitated, and she wondered if he was going to ask why she'd left, but he seemed to think better of it and moved on. Very little escaped Payson's sharp intellect; she suspected he guessed her reasons.

"It was only through luck that I discovered your dream to work in public relations. That's when the idea for the resort was born."

Harriet's jaw dropped. She snapped it shut. "You've got to be kidding me. You built the resort so you'd have a reason to hire me? That's-that's crazy ridiculous." It was beyond crazy.

She leaned toward him. "That's insane, Payson. Why not just offer me a job at one of your million other businesses?"

He rubbed his jaw and grimaced. "I needed you near so we could become friends. I moved to the island full time after my sister died and I didn't want to leave. This was her favorite of our homes and where I feel closest to her memory. This is where she's buried."

He shrugged. "I visit her grave almost daily," he admitted. "So I had to find a reason for you to move here."

Harriet sat back and shook her head. "I can't believe you built an entire resort so I would move to the island."

"It's only money, Harry. What point is there in having it if I don't use it to do what I want? The resort turned out to be a good thing. The workers here are happy and well compensated. Look at your orphan program. That's a resounding success, and something Penny would have approved of."

"But, Payson, I never applied for the position of public relations director. It was far above my experience level." She couldn't get past that point. In her experience, there was only one way to land a job; you applied for it and tried to convince the person doing the hiring that you were the best candidate.

"No, you didn't apply for the position. That's true. I miscalculated there. You forced me to find a way to make it impossible for you to turn down my offer."

Understanding dawned, and with it anger mixed with admiration. She had been manipulated every step of the way. Payson had set up a con and she had been the ignorant mark.

"You hired my closest friend," she accused.

"Yes. But unlike you, your friend applied to work here, and you should know that Solomon made the final cut on his own merit. The man is a botany genius. I fully expect him to create several new hybrids in his lifetime."

Harriet thought back to Solly's latest efforts and grimaced inwardly. She studied Payson. He looked tired. Had he lost sleep waiting to hear from her? The thought made her feel guilty.

"I'll be happy to share any memories of Penny as they return," she told him. "I've had a few flashes of life in the cult: picking apples with my father, racing my friend Danny up the hill. It's only been a few days and they've been crazy days. I'm sure more will come to me over time."

"Thank you for that. You're a kind and generous woman, Harry. I can see why Penny loved you." His gaze searched her face. "Are we good? Friends again?"

"Definitely." Harriet stood. She needed to get Belle home and feed her. She wanted to get in touch with Alex and find out where they stood on the search for the missing guests.

"Tag me after you've read the diaries. I'd like to talk about them. Plus I think talking will help me remember more." She headed for the door and stopped.

"Oh, one more thing," she said, turning to look at him.

Payson was fingering the top diary. She knew he was anxious to dig into them. He looked at her with a wary expression. She could almost see him wondering what more she could possibly have in store for him. She didn't wait for him to ask.

"In case you hadn't noticed, I have a dog now." She slipped through the door with Belle on her heels before he could respond. As she closed the door behind her she heard a soft chuckle and smiled to herself. Payson wouldn't be sending Belle away.

"Come on, Miss Belle. Let's get you some dinner and find Alex."

CHAPTER ELEVEN

Harriet found Alex sitting with Solly, William, and Tarbell on
Venus Cottage's lanai, eating noodles with fried vegetables that
Solly had whipped up. She fed Belle and grabbed a glass of white
wine before going out to join them.

"You didn't find the missing women, I take it." She edged
Alex's legs over and sat beside him on the lounger. He offered her
a forkful of noodles, but she shook her head. "Payson fed me
tomato soup and a grilled cheese sandwich. Eat. You need your
strength."

"Ah. Your talk went well, then."

Harriet gave a quick nod. She didn't want to share her
conversation with Payson in front of William and Tarbell.

"No sign of the missing women," Solly confirmed. "We were
just discussing our next move."

"Is there any possibility an employee took them and is hiding
them in his quarters? I hate to think a co-worker could be
responsible for the kidnappings, but if we've searched everywhere else . . ." Harriet didn't finish her thought. It would be
beyond awful if an employee had kidnapped the missing women.

"I can't see it," Alex said, "although we'd be remiss if we skipped searching all of the rooms on the resort, so it's next on the list."

"It feels unlikely to me too." Solly set his nearly empty dish down for Belle to lick clean. Much to Harriet's surprise, Belle hesitated and looked at her for permission.

"Go ahead, Belle. Good girl." Belle surged forward. The few morsels of food disappeared in an instant.

"It would help if we knew why those two women were taken," Solly continued. "Is it someone with a blonde fetish or do the women have something else in common?"

"They're from different cities. Different parts of the country even. I'm not sure what they could have in common besides money," Tarbell pointed out.

Harriet frowned at him. "I wouldn't be so quick to say that. They could belong to some nationwide group with local chapters. Or an online group, like a book club. Maybe they shop the same online store and a store employee saw their photos and decided he had to have them."

Solly rolled his eyes at her. "How likely is it that a store employee could get a reservation at this resort exactly the same week as Patricia and Azzi, let alone afford to come here?"

"There is that. I'm just saying, the women could have something more in common than their credit accounts."

"We might never find the connection if it's something like that," Tarbell pointed out. "We don't have enough information about their personal lives, and the friends they came to the resort with haven't been much help."

Harriet looked at Alex. "You're awfully quiet. What do you think?"

"I think you are absolutely right, that there has to be a connection between the two women, no matter how nebulous it might be. Unfortunately, Tarbell is also right—there's no one to ask. They don't have—" He stopped and swore under his breath.

"What a blasted idiot I am. Both women are alone in the world except for friends. Both inherited their family's money and possessions. I knew that, but I dismissed it because that means there's no one left to pay a ransom."

"Unless they buy their own freedom," Solly said. He pointed his fork at Alex. "Maybe we've found our motive."

"That would mean they're still alive, right?" Harriet looked at Alex. "Right?"

His mouth flattened.

"Not necessarily. The kidnappers could kill them once they have the ransom. Especially if the women saw their faces. Or the women could refuse to pay." They looked at each other with glum faces.

Harriet knew the men were frustrated by their lack of progress, but she also sensed a faint air of defeat that surprised her.

"We need to find them," she said. "We can't give up. Those two women are somewhere on this island and it's our responsibility to find where they're being kept."

"Right-O," Tarbell answered. "So, employee quarters next. Might as well hit those when we finish dinner. What about the greenhouses and laundry?"

"I checked the greenhouses. There's too much activity and no out of the way places to hide a person, let alone two, without being seen," Solly told him.

Alex nodded toward a figure on the beach walking in their direction. "Isn't that your friend, Martin O'Claire?" Harriet's head whipped around.

"I've only spoken to him briefly once or twice. That doesn't make us friends."

Alex shrugged. "He seems nice enough. He has one of the cottages on Blackbeard's Cove. Offered to lend us a hand searching after I looked through his place. Looks like he's coming this way."

"This seems like a good time to put some dessert together. Anyone need coffee?" William jumped up and disappeared inside Solly's cottage. Harriet hoped he had some of his mocha pinwheel cookies on hand. They were one of her favorites.

"Evening, everyone. Mind if I join you for a few minutes?"

"Of course not. Pull up a seat." Solly nodded toward the steps. "My partner's just gone inside for dessert and coffee. Can I get you a cup?"

"No. Thank you, though. That's very kind of you. I'm just stretching my legs, saw you all sitting here. Never could resist a gathering."

"Do you feel the need to see if we have any souls that need saving?"

Surprised at his caustic tone, Harriet looked at Tarbell. She hadn't realized he had issues with religion. Martin seemed unfazed, however.

"I don't go looking for lost souls, Mr. –?"

"Fox. Tarbell Fox. I thought it was every preacher's duty to be on the lookout for those who don't buy into their religious dogma."

"Tarbell!" Harriet gave him a dark look. "Don't be rude."

Martin waved a hand at her and chuckled."It's quite all right, Miss Monroe. Everyone is entitled to their opinion. Makes the world more interesting, as far as I'm concerned.

"As for religion, some believe in a higher power, some demand proof, and some have no need for it in their lives–they're perfectly happy giving it no thought. It's not my place to judge. I only try to be there if they want to talk."

Tarbell gave a disbelieving grunt but didn't pursue the subject, much to Harriet's relief. That he had a problem with either religion in general or preachers in particular was obvious. He was usually polite to everyone, no matter how irritating they were. She searched for a new topic.

"So, Mr. O'Claire, Alex tells me you own a home security company. That must be . . . interesting," she finished lamely. She wished she'd kept her mouth shut.

O'Claire's silvery gray eyes twinkled. "Call me Martin, please. Few industries are more staid and boring than home security, but I've done well enough. What did you do before you came to work here, Miss Monroe?"

"I worked for a small ad agency in the northeast." Harriet really didn't want to say any more about her life before the resort in case someone questioned why she'd been hired. Even though Payson had assured her she did an excellent job, she still felt a bit like an imposter. She took Alex's empty plate and stood.

"I'm going to see if William needs help in the kitchen. Excuse me."

William was nowhere to be seen when Harriet entered the kitchen. Thinking he might have paid a visit to the bathroom, she checked the coffee maker and saw he hadn't started it yet, so she scooped and measured the ground beans, added water, and turned it on. There was still no sign of William by the time she'd finished.

Concerned that the pastry chef might have fallen ill, Harriet went to the bedroom door to check on him. She found him standing just beyond the window edge, staring at the lanai.

"William? Are you okay?" He jerked hard at the sound of her voice and grabbed at the window frame to steady himself.

"Sorry. I came in to give you a hand with coffee and . . ." Her voice trailed off. William was staring out the window again.

"I'm fine," he answered without looking at her.

"You don't look fine. What's wrong?" He didn't look at all good; his normally pale skin looked positively white and clammy, and his breathing came in short, rapid bursts.

She took a step into the room. It was an exact mirror of her own bedroom, with a king-sized bed surrounded by white mosquito netting, a long, low dresser with cushioned chairs set against the wall on either side, and dark red-brown mahogany walls and floor. Through the open door opposite, she could make out a small bit of the mosaic scene on the bathroom ceiling and the glass-walled shower.

"William," she spoke softly, as if trying to coax a wild creature to trust her. "I know something's wrong. Please talk to me. I'll help in any way I can. Are you . . . Are you having a panic attack?"

"There's nothing you can do, Harry, but thank you." He looked at her then. She wanted to weep at the anger and desperation she saw in his eyes. "You've been very kind to me." He looked back out the window, dismissing her.

It wasn't her place to push and she didn't know William well enough to read the sub-text that takes place in every conversation.

"I'll just get the coffee then. Will you be joining us?"

"In a minute."

Harriet waffled for a long, awkward moment, debating whether or not to push him, then backed out of the bedroom and returned to the kitchen. She poured coffee for everyone, set the mugs on a tray, and headed back out to the lanai.

"Where's Will?" Solly asked as he took a mug from the offered tray.

"He said he'd be right out." She gave him a look that said all was not well. Solly frowned at her but got the message.

"I'd better check to see if Will needs my help with dessert." He set his mug on the deck beneath his lounger, but before he could rise, William appeared in the kitchen door with a platter of baked goods.

"There you are. We were beginning to think you'd absconded with dessert," Solly joked. He leaped to his feet and took the tray from William. "Let me help you with that."

Harriet finished handing out the coffee and joined Alex on his lounger.

"Where's Mr. O'Claire?" she asked, sniffing her coffee. The dark, nutty brew smelled wonderful.

"He decided to head back before it got too dark," Tarbell answered. "How about handing some of those pastries over here, Sol? I need to carb up if I'm going to be searching for missing women all night."

"Dibs on the pinwheels," Harriet said quickly, noting that there were only four on the tray. She could easily eat a dozen of the flaky chocolate pastry with coffee cream swirls without breaking a sweat. Tarbell grumbled something about first come, first serve, but he left the pinwheels for her.

Conversation gradually ceased. Everyone was tired and conserving energy for the night ahead. Harriet leaned back against Alex's chest and sipped her coffee, contentedly watching the sun touch the edge of the water, painting it a brilliant red and gold. The tide was caught in that quiet moment when it turns, and the breeze had stopped in tandem with the water.

"I feel as if we're in limbo," she said, breaking the quiet. "Like something is waiting to happen and we don't have a clue what, so we wait."

"Sometimes waiting is all we can do," Tarbell said. "Although I prefer action myself. Speaking of." He got to his feet. "Thanks for the vittles. I'm headed to the employee apartments to make their evenings."

"Give me a minute and I'll join you." Alex handed Harriet his coffee mug, picked her up and turned her on his lap, and kissed her.

"I want you to get some sleep. You're still running on a deficit. I'll be home after Tarbell and I search the employee housing." He pressed a finger to Harriet's lips when she tried to protest.

"Sleep. You need it. Now let me up. The sooner we conduct this search the sooner I can join you."

Harriet pushed herself off the lounger. She felt exhausted and wanted nothing more than to crawl into her bed, but she also felt as if she should be helping with the search. She staggered slightly when she got to her feet.

"Bed, Harriet. I mean it."

"Okay. Okay," she grumbled. She hated being told what to do. "I'll just give Solly a hand with the dishes and then I'll go to bed. I promise."

Alex looked at Solly. "Make sure our girl gets to bed, will you please?" He planted a kiss on Harriet's forehead and disappeared around the corner of the cottage after Tarbell.

"Let's get these done," Harriet said, gathering the mugs. "I didn't want to admit it, but Alex was right, I'm about running on empty."

Solly smirked. "You don't have to say anything. It shows." Harriet stuck her tongue out and carried the mugs into the kitchen where she found William already loading the dinner dishes into the dishwasher.

"Will has this. Set down the mugs and I'll escort you and Belle to your cottage."

"Sol, it's right next door. I'm sure I can make it on my own that far."

"Really? And yet Alex asked me to see that you got to bed. So that is what I am going to do. Come on."

"Good night, William," Harriet called as Solly gently pushed hert out the door. "Dessert was wonderful."

Solly waited until they were inside Mermaid Cottage before turning on her. "What was that look when you came out with the coffee? What happened with Will?"

"He was in the bedroom when I went in to help him, just staring out the window. He looked pretty shook up. His skin was pale and he was breathing hard, like he was having a panic attack."

Solly rubbed the back of his neck. "Maybe he *was* having an anxiety attack. It's possible, although I've never seen him have one before. He's pretty shy. Maybe sitting around with all of us was too much for him."

Harriet gave it some thought. "Poor guy. He must have been embarrassed when I caught him. If he'll talk to you about it, tell him I don't think any less of him. Lots of people suffer from them. I'm told they can be quite scary, even feel like a heart attack."

Solly kissed her on the cheek. "Thank you for caring. Now go to bed. You look like shit."

"Jerk."

"Brat." They smiled fondly at each other. Harriet locked the door and set the alarm behind him, took a quick shower, and was soon sound asleep.

She had no idea how long she'd been asleep when something awakened her. Harriet opened her eyes and tried to orient herself in the dark. The moon either hadn't risen yet, or there was no moon—she couldn't remember which it was.

Her eyes closed and she began to drift off again, but a low growl from Belle's throat made her jerk up in bed.

"Belle, what is it?" Unwilling to turn on a light and risk losing her night vision, Harriet strained to see the dog in the room's shadows. She eventually made out Belle's bulky form beside the bed. The dog was staring at the lanai glass doors. A low growl emitted from her deep chest.

Harriet began to inch toward the edge of the bed, but shrank back when a thin beam of light suddenly swept the room.

Someone was on her lanai. Someone who was using a penlight to look inside her cottage.

Harriet rolled to the opposite side of the bed, away from the glass doors. She crawled out from under the insect netting and dropped to the floor. The beam of light winked out as suddenly as it had appeared.

While she lay there, her bare flesh pressed to the cool wood, she tried to remember where she'd left her clothes.

Belle gave another menacing growl.

Harriet crawled on her hands and knees to the chair where Alex kept his sweatpants and a tee shirt, his preferred loungewear. Lying on her back, she hastily pulled them on, then got to her feet, gripping the pants with one hand to keep them from falling to her knees.

Through the bedroom door she saw the beam of light flash across the living room, then wink out.

Right. Someone was casing her cottage. If it was the kidnapper then this was her chance to identify him. She tiptoed to the lanai doors.

"Belle. Stay with me." Harriet unlocked and quietly slid open the left-hand door and slipped outside. She caught a brief glimpse of a figure by the kitchen doors, peering in.

Belle began to bark. The intruder glanced her way and took off around the corner of the cottage. She heard feet pounding sand, then nothing.

"Stop!" Harriet started after him but forgot she had to hold up Alex's pants and they tangled in her feet. She went down hard, bruising a knee and an elbow.

"Dammit." There was no point in trying to follow. He would have too much of a lead, especially hampered as she was by the too big sweatpants.

Had that been the kidnapper, after another blonde?

"He must have been surprised to find a dog guarding me," Harriet told Belle. "Come on. I think you need a treat as your reward and I need to call Alex. Apparently our kidnapper isn't finished."

CHAPTER TWELVE

Alex roared up on the Triumph ten minutes after Harriet called him. He found her sitting at her pink granite kitchen island, every light in the cottage blazing, her hands wrapped around a cup of hot tea to keep them from shaking.

The shakes hadn't set in until after she had called Alex. She knew they were caused by a combination of exhaustion and after-adrenalin rush, but they made her feel weak, which in turn made her cross and short-tempered. Anger was better than fear anytime. It didn't help that he'd been cross-examining her almost from the moment he walked in the door.

"Are you sure you didn't see anything more?" Alex sounded as frustrated as she felt. He paced from the lanai to the island and loomed over her.

"I stepped onto the lanai from the bedroom. I saw a figure peering in the kitchen doors. It was dark, and whoever it was, was wearing dark clothes and a dark hat pulled over his hair. *That's all I saw.* You didn't see anyone on the road on your way here?"

"No." Clearly agitated, Alex pushed his fingers through his

thick, black hair. "Tell me again. Belle woke you up. She was growling."

"I've already told you," Harriet snapped. They were both silent for a long moment.

"Sorry." She rubbed her forehead with her fingers. "I didn't see anything that will help."

"Tell me again, anyway. Please."

She took a deep breath, and as patiently as she could, related the events for the dozenth time. Each time, Alex hoped she would remember some new detail, but it had been too dark and she hadn't seen enough, plain and simple.

The shadow of a person peering in her bedroom window. A brief glimpse at a dark figure at the kitchen doors. The beam of a penlight sweeping her bedroom and then the living room while she cowered on the floor. It could have been any tall male guest. Or even a co-worker. She shied away from that last thought.

She knew it was the fact that she had cowered instead of rushing out to confront the creep that angered her the most. That, and the fact that she hadn't chased him.

Alex took off the leather jacket he wore when riding his bike, tossed it on a stool, and pulled his link from his pocket.

"Fox. Yeah, it looks like our kidnapper was thinking of making a run at Harriet. I can't leave her here alone. Can you finish up there? Yeah, good. I really didn't expect to find anything. Go home and get some sleep. Meet me at the office at seven. I'll fill you in then." He cut the call and turned to find Harriet scowling at him.

"You have a job to do, Alex. Go do it. I don't need a babysitter. I have Belle to protect me. Besides, it's unlikely the kidnapper would dare to come back here tonight."

"Nope. Ain't gonna happen." He poured a glass of water from the chiller and drank it down. "Besides, Fox is almost finished searching the employee apartments. Come on, let's go to bed. At least I'll get a good night's rest out of this."

Harriet knew Alex wasn't angry with her–he was angry at himself because he hadn't been here to protect her. She couldn't help but wonder what would have happened if Belle hadn't been with her tonight.

For those reasons, and because it was obvious the kidnapper wasn't done, she didn't offer any further argument. She took Alex's hand and led him to the bedroom where they held each other tight.

She thought she'd lie awake the rest of the night, but she fell asleep almost as soon as her head hit the pillow.

The previous night's Peeping Tom felt more like a bad dream with the morning sunshine flooding Mermaid Cottage. Harriet skipped her run since Alex didn't have time to run with her and he wouldn't let her go alone, despite her argument that she'd take Belle with her.

They argued after that, one of their few real fights. Alex insisted Harriet accompany him to his office and remain there until he could escort her to her own office. She accused him of not trusting her to take care of herself and insisted the kidnapper wouldn't dare try to take her in broad daylight. They glared at each other, neither wanting to cede their position.

After ten minutes of stomping around the cottage, Alex grabbed Harriet by the waist and pulled her to him.

"You promise to keep Belle with you every moment?" Harriet nodded.

"Yes."

"And you'll remain locked in the cottage with the alarm on until it's time to go to work? No sitting on the lanai?"

She huffed about it, but eventually gave in.

"I don't want to fight. And I don't want anything to happen to you. You've been through enough. These last few days . . . They've been more than most people experience in a lifetime."

Harriet softened. "I know you're feeling protective. I don't want anything to happen to me either. I'll be uber careful, I promise."

Alex brushed the hair back from her face and kissed her. "You'd better," he murmured, "or I might end up serving time for murder if I catch the person who dares to harm you."

Harriet locked up and set the alarm behind him as promised and then wondered what to do with herself. She'd missed her morning run and hated being stuck inside when she wanted to drink her coffee on the lanai.

She stood in the kitchen and looked out the window, the same window the Peeping Tom had been peering in when she accosted him.

Him. She kept thinking of the peeper as a man. Apparently her subconscious recognized the person as male. He'd been tall and moved like an athlete. Why would a kidnapper be interested in her? If he was after ransoms then he was barking up the wrong tree.

Although come to think of it, her ex-fiancé's estate would be settled soon and she was the sole beneficiary.

She shook her head. Bradley had been well off, but not what anyone would consider wealthy.

"They better find this guy fast," Harriet grumbled to Belle, "or you're going to hear a lot more fighting. Let's go to work. I hate hanging around." She grabbed Belle's makeshift leash and her canvas pack and headed off.

The island looked and sounded and smelled exactly as it did every other morning. Drops of dew dripped from green leaves and sparkled on colorful flowers that perfumed the air. The jungle's denizens buzzed, sang, and chirped while they went about the daily business of mating and finding food. A few guests walked the beach below the shell road.

There was no outward sign that something ugly was happening beneath the friendly facade of the resort.

She caught sight of Fitness Couple running side by side down the beach, their arms and legs moving in perfect unison.

"They are so weird," she told Belle, who was more interested in a large lizard watching them from the underbrush. "They're almost like clones."

Could Fitness Guy be their kidnapper? He was certainly athletic enough. If he was the kidnapper, then where was he hiding the women? And what about Fitness Gal? Was she part of it?

Harriet watched until they shrank to miniature people, still chugging along in unison. She tried to picture them as a kidnapping couple, but it didn't work for her. Fitness Couple were classic narcissists. They didn't have the brain bandwidth to think about anyone else.

Several employees going about their daily tasks stopped her to ask about the missing guests. No one appeared upset over having their quarters searched and all volunteered to help if a larger search became necessary. Harriet thanked them and promised she'd tell Alex.

When she entered her office lobby, Jeeves looked alarmed at the sight of Belle. She hadn't considered that he might never have seen a dog before.

"There is a beast on your tail, Miss Harry," the droid pointed out. "Should I do something about it?"

It had never occurred to Harriet that her office droid might possess the same fighting capabilities as Alex's Mary. For one thing, the two droid models were like night and day. They couldn't look or act more different from one another.

With his handsome good looks and perfectly folded handkerchief peeking from the breast pocket of his neatly pressed suit, Jeeves always looked like the historic proper English gentleman he was modeled after, and his pleasant demeanor and British accent never failed to charm Harriet.

She gave him a big smile and introduced him to Belle. He froze for a moment while he accessed his data files on dogs, then held out his hand for Belle to sniff. Harriet wondered what a droid smelled like. They wouldn't possess the normal physical odors that every human carried around with them. Plastics and metal, perhaps?

The thought saddened her. Jeeves seemed as real as a–well, a real human. She'd even come to think of him as a friend.

She had grown up with droids. Everyone did. They were commonly employed as household staff. They manned retail counters, worked in factories, maintenance, security–in short, they were everywhere.

Once the initial investment was made, the only cost to owning a droid was a yearly maintenance check-up and the electricity to recharge them. She'd never owned one herself, but her ex had used three to keep his Eastern Promenade mansion and yard looking pristine.

The resort's droids were the top of the line. They worked as sous chefs alongside the humans in the kitchens. They worked at the marina and the amusement park and circus. But the office droids–Mary and Jeeves–were special. She wondered if Jeeve's model was even available to the public. Since Payson owned the lab that developed the best droids, it made sense that he would test them first.

She watched to make sure Belle didn't try to harm Jeeves, but Belle gave the droid a brief sniff and then ignored him. She circled the room, sniffing the floor and furniture.

"I must order dog treats to give Belle when she visits with you," Jeeves said. "My research tells me that it is customary."

"I'm sure Belle would be most appreciative. She has a bottomless pit." Seeing the confusion on Jeeves' face, Harriet explained. "She's always hungry."

She saw Jeeves file away the popular expression. His slang vocabulary had grown since being activated for the office. She'd even caught him trying a few out on her. She knew droids didn't experience emotions, but she swore it gave him pleasure when he got something right.

"I have a message for you from Mr. Hayes," Jeeves said. "I am to inform you that you must keep the doors to your lanai locked while you are in the office and I am to inform him if you open them."

"Great." What was the point of having an office that overlooked the beach if she couldn't open the doors to enjoy the sea breeze? Feeling very much like an innocent prisoner, Harriet led Belle down the corridor to her office and let herself in.

After setting a bowl of water down for Belle, Harriet picked up the holo of her parents and wished them a good morning. They smiled out at her, perpetually happy in the moment the holo had been taken; a moment she now knew was before they joined the Cult of the Blissed.

Her parents had wanted to do good in the world, had wanted to do no harm to the planet. Both parents had taught her to honor and care for the natural world. Her mother even refused to kill spiders, preferring to capture them and set them loose outside their longhouse.

It was a good memory, one that made Harriet smile. She could remember another woman, one with dark curly hair, shrieking with laughter when they found a harmless garter snake curled up inside a cooking pot. Harriet had been fascinated by the snake's long yellow and black stripes and had begged her mother to let her keep it as a pet.

The other woman must have been Penelope, she realized with a jolt. That would have been when Payson's sister first joined the cult and shared her family's longhouse, before she moved into Mayo's place.

She remembered Penny now; always smiling and always willing to help out with whatever needed to be done. Penny used to tell her stories about her travels with her big brother.

She would have to remember to tell Payson about the memories. He would like knowing that his sister had laughed and was happy.

Harriet set the holo back on the shelf and sat at her desk, but concentrating on her latest ad campaign proved impossible. She had too many other things crowding her brain. She went to stand by the lanai doors, wishing she could open them. Belle stretched out on one of the scatter rugs and began to softly snore.

A knock at the door startled them both. How long had she been standing there daydreaming? Belle gave a woof, lumbered to her feet, and stared at the door expectedly. Since the door to the office corridor was kept locked at all times, and Jeeves stood guard, Harriet had a good idea who had come to pay a visit. She walked over to the door and hit the control. The door slid openly silently.

"Come on in, Cassie." The resort's manager filled the doorway. Dressed in one of her many billowing caftans, this one a deep green with large, pale yellow flowers, Cassandra Montgomery pushed past Harriet and made a beeline for Belle.

Although twenty years older than Harriet, the two women had become good friends. Harriet admired Cassie's quick intelligence and her complete acceptance of herself. While most women would be constantly dieting and dressing in black to look thinner, Cassie dressed her large figure in brightly colored caftans and never pretended to be trying to lose weight.

"I heard you brought a dog back from the mainland. I couldn't believe it. Aren't you a beautiful girl," she cooed, rubbing Belle's ears. The dog leaned into Cassie's legs and closed her eyes in bliss.

Harriet shook her head in disgust. How much protection could Belle offer if the dog sucked up to anyone willing to rub her ears?

Cassie straightened and gave Harriet a worried look. "What do you think about the missing women? I'm going to meet with Alex and Tarbell later to discuss adding more security. We can't ignore the need any longer. If the guests don't feel safe here they'll eventually stop coming."

"Obviously I want them to be found unharmed and alive. Other than that, I don't know what to think, Cass."

"Don't we all." Cassie walked over to Harriet's seating arrangement and plunked her bulk into a pale peach cushioned chair, a sure sign that this wasn't going to be a quick visit.

That was fine with Harriet. She wasn't getting anything done anyway and it would be good to hear the manager's point of view about the disappearances. She poured two orange natural flavored fizzy waters, handed one to Cassie, and took a seat opposite the resort manager. They talked about the resort's lack of security cameras, the missing women, and the way the resort had become a magnet for murder.

"I had a Peeping Tom last night." Harriet hadn't intended to say anything. The words had just popped out of her mouth.

Cassie looked appropriately shocked. "What happened? Was Alex there?"

"No. Alex and Tarbell were searching employee housing. Belle woke me and we frightened him off. I didn't get a good look at him. He was peering in my windows and he had a flashlight. I don't know if he was looking for me or if he was casing the place to rob it." Robbery didn't make any sense. Other than her collection of hand carved, miniature wooden hippos, she didn't own anything of value.

Cassie narrowed her eyes. "The two missing women are both blondes. You're a blonde. What if he was planning to kidnap you too?"

"I almost wish he had succeeded. Then at least I'd know what's going on."

"You don't mean that."

"No," Harriet admitted, "I don't, but Alex has nothing. It's as if the women were spirited from their beds and transported off the island. No one saw or heard anything. One of the guests saw Patricia Williams getting something from the hotel lobby refreshment bar in the early morning on the day she disappeared. That's it. How is our kidnapper taking them without anyone seeing? Where are they being kept?"

"Don't ask me. My brain doesn't do nefarious." Cassie took a delicate sip of the water. "I'm more sunshine, ice cream, and puppy dogs. Speaking of puppies, that's quite the dog you brought back with you. Where'd you find her?"

Harriet hesitated. She had never discussed her missing years with Cassie. Believing her memories had been wiped because her first eight years were too horrific to handle, she had kept her amnesia a secret from all but a couple of people. Perhaps now there wasn't any further need to be so secretive.

Except there was the news media. They would love to get hold of the only survivor of the mass suicide that was now a mass murder. Cassie wouldn't necessarily go to the media with the story, but Harriet knew that the more people who shared a secret, the more likely that secret would leak.

"Her owner's house burned down and the owner died. There

wasn't anyone to take Belle and I didn't have the heart to drop her off at a shelter." It was the truth, just not the whole truth.

"You're a good soul, Harry. Now about our missing women–"

Harriet's link buzzed before Cassie could finish her thought.

"It's Alex."

"Answer it, girl. Maybe he has news."

Alex had news all right, just not what they'd hoped to hear.

"Where are you?" he demanded.

"In my office. Cassie's here."

"Don't leave. I'm on my way to pick you up." He sounded angry and worried. Harriet gave Cassie a puzzled look. She knew Alex had no reason to be angry with her.

"Alex, what's going on? What's happened?"

"Angela Daly is missing."

Harriet's hand flew to her heart. "Oh, no. When?"

"About an hour ago. Her boyfriend just reported it. Fox says you helped him search their room."

Tarbell's grim face appeared on the screen.

"You remember Angela, Harry. You know her as Fitness Girl."

CHAPTER THIRTEEN

Cassie stayed with Harriet until Alex showed up. He didn't have any more information to share, except to assure Cassie he didn't think she was in any danger as their kidnapper appeared to prefer young blondes and Cassie was a brunette.

After he loaded Belle into the back seat of the Hog, he pulled Harriet in for a fierce hug. She knew he needed the comfort and waited until she felt his body relax slightly before she pushed away enough to search his face.

"I saw them running together when I walked to work this morning," she told him. "Angela can't have been missing for more than a few hours. What happened?"

"I don't know yet. I sent Fox to the hotel to interview Angela's roommate. He's waiting for me there. I –" He stopped and took a deep breath.

"I need you to stick with me. The kidnapper's growing bolder. Taking a woman in broad daylight . . ." He shook his head. "I don't want you to be alone until this is over. I can't do my job if I'm worrying over whether you're safe or not."

Harriet knew he was upset over the missing women and afraid for her, so she didn't argue. Truth be told, given her

Peeping Tom and the latest kidnapping, she didn't want to be alone.

"All right. What do you suggest?"

Alex pulled her back in. "Thank you for not fighting me on this. We'll head to the hotel and speak with Rodney Lynch first and then decide how to proceed. One step at a time."

They found Rodney Lynch sitting ramrod straight on the loveseat in the sitting room with Fox leaning against the wall next to the bedroom door, watching him. The room was pristine, no clothes or dirty dishes lying around.

Fox pushed away from the wall and nodded toward Rodney.

"I wouldn't let him say anything, Boss. Thought it would be better if we heard it for the first time together."

"Appreciate it." Alex guided Harriet to a cushioned chair off to one side, pulled a hardback chair from the dining table, turned it, and sat facing the back. Tarbell remained standing. They all focused on Rodney, who looked remarkably calm to Harriet considering his girlfriend was missing. His moss green eyes regarded them calmly.

"Walk me through it, Rodney," Alex said.

"We went for a run, same as we do every morning." His voice was level, as if he was reciting a business report. "We returned to the hotel. Angie wanted to ask the desk clerk about the mystery dinner theatre. I came up here to shower. When I came out of the bathroom she still wasn't back, so I went down to the lobby to look for her."

"Where did you run and what time did you return?"

"The south end of the island, past the greenhouses. We got back at exactly eight-thirty, like we do every morning. We pride ourselves on keeping to a strict schedule."

"And that was the last time you saw or heard from Angela?"

"Yes."

Harriet turned her wrist slightly so she could see her watch.

Angela had been missing for two and a half hours. She frowned. Why had it taken so long for Rodney to report her missing? Apparently Tarbell wondered the same thing.

"You waited quite a while to report your girlfriend's disappearance. Why was that?" he asked.

"She's not my girlfriend." Harriet detected something wistful in his voice. She thought of Angela standing in the bedroom doorway dressed only in a thong. Despite Rodney's claim, they were definitely more than friends.

"I thought she might have headed to the restaurant to check on the dinner show," Rodney continued. "Angie likes to have all the facts before she makes a decision."

"What do you and Miss Daly do for work, Mr. Lynch?" Harriet glanced apologetically at Alex. She knew she was meant to be an observer only, but her curiosity got the better of her.

Rodney turned his head to look at her. "We're licensed companions," he said. The corners of his full lips turned up in an attractive smile.

Suddenly the perfectly tuned bodies made sense. Licensed companions were at the top of the sex worker pyramid. They were strictly monitored and checked monthly for disease, were well trained in the art of giving pleasure, and were intelligent and well-read. They were the perfect companion for hire with no strings attached.

They were also very well paid for their time and their client lists often included politicians and the movers and shakers of the world—in short, the very people who made up the resort's guest list.

"Are you and Angela Daly more than co-workers, Mr. Lynch?" Alex looked pointedly at the door next to Tarbell. "It appears that you're sleeping in the same bed. I assume you are in a relationship of some kind."

"We're friends and occasional sex partners. Sometimes we

work together. We aren't sharing the same room on this trip. Angie has a tendency to spread out and I hate clutter." Rodney shrugged.

"The money making years for a licensed companion are short. We're both focused on milking our careers for all we can. Neither of us is interested in a monogamous relationship at this time, so no. We are not more than co-workers."

Harriet thought she caught a bitter undernote even though his tone remained even. She felt a twinge of sympathy. The money-making years for a licensed companion coincided with the prime dating-leading-to-family-building years, but most people had a problem sharing their spouse with a string of strangers. It had to be a lonely life.

Alex nodded. "All right. She wasn't here after you showered. What did you do then?"

"I got dressed and went down to check the lobby. She wasn't there either so I walked over to the restaurant, but the doors were locked."

"Did you try tagging her link?" Tarbell asked.

"No. We leave them in the suite when we run."

"Maybe Angela came back for hers while you were in the shower. Give her a call."

Rodney walked over to the kitchenette counter and picked up a leopard print link. A moment later a ringtone sounded from the bedroom. He set the link back on the counter and returned to his seat.

Alex jerked his head toward the bedroom door. Tarbell disappeared for a minute and returned holding a slim black unit.

"Is this Angela's link?" he asked, showing it to Rodney.

"Yes."

Harriet studied Rodney's profile. He sat stiffly and didn't fidget. A small tic toward the back of his jaw was the only sign she could find that he might be upset. Whether the tic was because of his roommate's disappearance or from being interviewed by two ex detectives, she couldn't tell.

"Had you and Angela discussed the missing women?" Alex asked.

"Of course. Angie wasn't worried. She can take care of herself. She trains in Krav Maga several days a week when we're at home." Seeing Harriet's puzzled frown he elaborated.

"Sometimes a client believes they have the right to do anything they want because they've bought our time, even when told no rough stuff. That's not our game, although other LCs are happy to provide that sort of service."

Harriet knew very little about Krav Maga, the self defense method developed almost two centuries earlier by Israeli Special Forces, but she was intrigued. She made a mental note to find a trainer. The way her life had been going, she could use some self defense skills.

"Look." Exasperation crossed Rodney's face for the first time since they'd entered the suite. "Angie wouldn't take off without telling me. She definitely wouldn't take off without a shower and clean clothes. She's a clean freak when it comes to her body. We'd just been for a run and we were sweaty. She was going to stop by the front desk and ask about the dinner mystery theater thing. Something is wrong."

"Mr. Lynch," Harriet said, "is it possible that one of Angela's clients is here on the island and recognized her? Maybe wanted another date and she refused?"

"If that's the case, I wouldn't know. Part of being a licensed companion is discretion. We don't share the names of our clients with anyone. I know the names of the ones we've worked together, of course, but we try not to discuss our work when we're off the clock."

Alex stood and returned his chair to the table.

"We'd like you to stay in your suite until one of us contacts you again," he said. "We'll talk to the front desk and ask around, see who noticed Angela after your run."

"I was going to snag some breakfast in the rooftop restaurant."

"Call room service. I want someone here in case your friend returns."

Rodney agreed, but he didn't look happy about it. Alex and Tarbell followed Harriet from the room. Once in the hall outside, they stopped.

"That was an excellent point about a past client possibly being involved," Tarbell told Harriet, speaking low so they wouldn't be heard. "I hadn't thought of that possibility, although I'm not sure how it would tie in to the two other missing women."

"I can't figure any connection either. It just occurred to me that their clients would be the same people who visit the resort." Harriet looked at Alex. "What do you think?"

He pinched the bridge of his nose and made a low huff of frustration. Dropping his hand, he shook his head.

"Damned if I know. Angela definitely fits the profile: attractive, young, and blonde. But it blows my theory that ransoms might be behind the kidnappings. I'm sure she makes excellent money, but I doubt that it's enough to pay a ransom. At least not one large enough to justify the risk of prison time. And does this have anything to do with the man peering in your windows last night?"

"I'll speak to the desk clerk," Tarbell said. "Then I'll start showing Angela's photo around to anyone in front of the hotel."

"Harriet and I are headed back to the office. I need to do a more thorough background check on our male guests. I'm missing something."

Harriet groaned. She didn't want to sit around Alex's bare office and watch him work.

"I'd rather go back to my office or help Tarbell."

"Harriet–" Alex didn't look happy. She crossed her arms over her chest.

"I can't sit around your office for hours doing nothing. I'll go stir crazy. Besides, whoever this kidnapper is, he's busy with Angela at the moment. I doubt very much that he's going to come after me today."

"She has a point, Alex."

"I know she does, dammit."

Harriet kissed his cheek. "Thank you. I'm going to help Tarbell. I'll call you if I go anywhere else." He didn't look happy, but he knew he'd gain nothing by arguing.

"Right. Let's figure this out. We have three missing women. They have to be somewhere." He ran lightly down the stairs with Harriet and Tarbell on his heels and left them in the lobby.

Tarbell shot the photo of Angela Daly to Harriet's link. They split up and worked the lobby, showing Angela's photo to the other guests, then walked outside to collect Belle from the Hog. The strip between the water and the hotel was busy with guests traveling back and forth, and most of the benches in front were occupied.

"I had a few guests ask me if they were in danger," Harriet told Tarbell. "I assured them they weren't, but to be honest, I'm not so sure I was telling the truth. What if our kidnapper starts going after older women, or brunettes or redheads?"

"Yeah, I fielded more questions this time too. I'm wondering if we should alert the guests to travel in pairs, or groups. Three missing women in as many days–our kidnapper is a busy boy. If we lose another guest we'll only have ourselves to blame."

"Good morning. And a fine one it is. How are you this morning, Miss Monroe? And Mr. Fox, is it?" Martin O'Claire stood behind them, rocking on his toes with his hands clasped behind his back.

How long had he been standing there? Harriet pasted a smile

on her face. It made her uncomfortable how often O'Claire turned up. Could he be their kidnapper? She narrowed her eyes and tried to imagine him peering into her windows in the dark.

It was possible. The man on her lanai had been taller than her. It was hard to say just how tall, since he'd been bent over peering into the kitchen, and then was gone.

O'Claire was as tall as Alex: around six-three, maybe six-four. She realized she'd been staring and turned away to free Belle from the Hog, but not before she caught the humor in O'Claire's eyes. She flushed. Did he think she was ogling him? The thought horrified her.

"What are you two up to this morning?" he asked.

"Searching for another missing woman," Tarbell answered curtly. He pulled out his link and showed it to O'Claire. "Have you seen this woman?

"Sure. I see her every day. She's a fitness freak. I see her running with her friend and sunning on the hotel loungers. She probably visits the spa every day as well." There was no mistaking the scorn in his voice.

Harriet didn't know why she felt the need to defend Angela, but she couldn't let O'Claire's judgemental tone pass.

"That's because her body is her livelihood, Mr. O'Claire. As a preacher, I would think you of all people would know better than to pass judgement before hearing the whole story." Harriet turned away and let Belle out of the Hog.

"I stand properly chastised. You're right. I have little patience with narcissists and I applied that label to your missing woman without looking deeper. Thank you for pointing that out to me, Miss Monroe." He inclined his head and strode off.

"Crap. I should have kept my mouth shut." Harriet slipped the lead over Belle's head and slammed the Hog's door.

"Forget it. Don't preachers talk about turning the other cheek? He'll get over it. And if he doesn't? You'll never have to see him again." He grinned. "Let's get to work. You take the people to the left of the lobby doors, I'll take the right." They split up. Fifteen minutes later they met at the Hog again.

"Anything?" Tarbell asked. Harriet shook her head.

"Most people knew Angela by sight but no one saw her after they left for their run this morning." A furrow appeared between Tarbell's brows.

"Same here. Which makes no sense. Darrin said Angela never stopped to ask about the dinner theatre, although he admits that he was busy with guests all morning and didn't see them return from their run."

Harriet stared at the water, thinking. "If someone took Angela against her will, people would have noticed. She would have put up a fight, especially if she has self defense training." She looked at Tarbell.

"That means she willingly went off with someone. Patricia and Azzi might have gone willingly with their kidnapper as well. What if the kidnapper is using a decoy–someone who is working with him?"

"You mean a woman." Tarbell pursed his lips. "It would explain a lot. Our victims wouldn't be alarmed if another woman approached them. I'm going to run that idea by Alex." He pulled out his link and placed the call.

"Alex. Harry wonders if we might be looking for a couple working together." He listened for a minute, then hung up.

"The boss says you're brilliant, but now he needs to expand his background checks so you're to stick with me."

"Great. What's next?"

"We head back to the amusement park, show Angela's photo around, and get something to eat. I'm famished. The boss hasn't found anything suspicious on any of our guests–at least nothing that makes him think they might be a kidnapper."

"Then we keep looking."

Tarbell nodded. "Yep. Let's get to the park."

Someone had removed the gag so she could drink. She'd been so thirsty she couldn't gulp the water fast enough and had ended up choking, with water dribbling down her chin and over her chest.

"What do you want with me?"

Her question was met with silence.

"Who are you?"

Nothing. Her pajamas were soiled and she stank. Her arms and legs felt numb. She hoped it wasn't permanent. She didn't know if her captor was a man or a woman. She felt a momentary embarrassment that a man would see her in that condition.

Patricia didn't think of herself as a fighter, but she tried to fight the gag when they put it back on—a losing battle with her hands tied. She made up her mind that she would give them whatever they wanted if they'd only let her go, but they didn't give her a chance to tell them that before the gag was back in place.

And then that prick, this time in the arm. The one that made her forget where she was.

She surrendered to the bliss.

CHAPTER FOURTEEN

As Harriet and Tarbell worked their way through the amusement park again, they learned that plenty of people had noticed Angela Daly, but no one had seen her after her and Rodney's morning run.

"Dejá vu."

"What?" They stood together outside the park gate.

"This is the third time we've done this in as many days," Harriet elaborated. "And we're no closer to figuring out who took those women. No one sees anything. No one hears anything. They're here and then they're not. It's as if someone waved a magic wand and Poof! They're gone. I'm frustrated, and to be honest, I'm a little frightened."

"They have to be somewhere. We'll find them."

"But will we find them in time?"

Tarbell didn't bother to answer her. How could he when he was thinking the same thing?

Harriet took the Hog back to Mermaid Cottage. When she arrived, she simply sat and stared at nothing. She felt untethered, as if she'd barely had a moment to catch her breath. The fire, the attempt on her life, learning that Payson's younger sister was the catalyst for a mass murder that included her parents. One, two, and now three, missing women. Alex's proposal.

Would her life ever settle into a comfortable groove again? If it did, she promised to never complain about being bored.

She shook off the melancholia and let Belle out. The dog had been a star all day, never complaining and staying close to Harriet while she and Tarbell questioned the guests about Angela. She was beginning to think that maybe she could handle owning a pet after all.

Belle loved the amusement park. Children (and even some adults) dropped food that barely hit the ground before she snatched it up, and she loved the pool at the base of the waterfall slide. Her tail wagged the entire time they were in the park, and Harriet swore she wore a grin on her beautiful big face.

She disarmed the cottage's alarm and Belle trotted inside, obviously recognizing after only a few days that this was her new home. It gave Harriet a warm and fuzzy feeling to hear Belle slurp water from the bowl she had left on the kitchen floor before padding back to the living room where she jumped up on the couch and immediately fell sleep.

Alex arrived on the Triumph before Harriet had even kicked off her shoes and hung up her canvas bag. She felt more warm and fuzzy feelings when he came through the door and pulled her in for a thorough kiss that left her somewhat breathless.

After he released her, he pulled four thumbnail-sized objects from his jacket pocket.

"What are those?"

"Cameras."

"Cameras? For what?"

"I'm going to set one up on each side of the cottage in case your Peeping Tom decides to return."

"I see. And who exactly will be monitoring these cameras?" She thought of the times she stepped outside in the underpants and tank top she preferred over pajamas. She didn't want Tarbell watching her.

"Only me. They're programmed to feed to my office comm unit and will only record any time there's movement. That way I won't have to sit through hours of nothing looking for something." He noticed the less than pleased look on Harriet's face and correctly guessed why it was there.

"They aren't permanent. Just until we catch our kidnapper and/or Peeping Tom. I know how you feel about privacy."

Harriet inspected one closely. "They're so small. Are you sure they'll work?"

"Positive. Payson got them for me. One of his labs builds miniature cams for the medical field–like the ones they use to look inside the body. These are prototypes for a new line of security cams that are supposed to shoot high definition even in low light. This is a test to see if they deliver the quality needed to actually ID someone well enough for an arrest and to stand up in court."

"As long as they're temporary. I don't want to feel as if someone is watching me every time I step outside."

He dropped a kiss on her nose. "Not to worry. Although I'm hoping Payson will let me install these in the hotel lobby when I'm finished with them here."

She could see the upside to the cameras. If they'd been installed yesterday they would have video of her Peeping Tom and might be closer to identifying him.

"I don't want you to mention the cameras to anyone, not even Solly."

"You can't believe that either Solly or William are my Peeping Tom. That's ridiculous. And Solly can keep a secret as well as anybody."

"I trust Solly. The jury's still out on William. I don't know him well enough to say I trust him without reservation, and I don't want to put Solly in the awkward position of having to lie to William. It's only for a few days. One way or the other, our kidnapper will be leaving on Saturday."

Harriet wasn't sure how she felt about that. On the one hand, the kidnapper wouldn't be able to cause any more trouble for them. On the other hand, what if they didn't have the women back by Saturday?

Alex pulled a small drill from another pocket and headed outside to install the miniature cameras. Harriet heard him whistling a minute later and shook her head. Alex loved gadgets. He was never going to give those cameras back to Payson.

A knock at the door interrupted her thoughts. When she opened it she found Payson standing there holding Margaret Blackstone's diaries.

"I should have called," he said.

"Nonsense. You're always welcome. Come in. I was just about to pour some wine and get Alex a beer. Which would you prefer?" Although she didn't care for beer herself, she made sure Alex's favorite brand was always stocked and cold in the chiller, especially now that he spent most nights at the cottage.

"Wine would be good." Payson followed her to the kitchen and set the diaries on the pink granite island. "Interesting reading. Margaret was extremely intelligent. You didn't tell me that she developed Blitz as a money maker for Mayo Sinclair. Or that members of the cult were leaving because of it."

Harriet set a glass of white wine in front of him. Leaning against the counter, she took a sip from her own glass before answering.

"It's not a pleasant story, is it? I wonder how many cult members agreed to help Mayo sell the drug? I don't think my parents or your sister would have hung around him for much longer. Mom and Dad were very concerned with clean living and all that entails: clean food, clean water, clean air. They wouldn't have liked the idea of selling an addictive drug–any drug–to fund their lifestyle."

"Penny would have felt the same. It's a shame they didn't get away before Margaret killed them."

Life was filled with if-onlys, but that was a big giant one. Maybe the biggest of all as far as Harriet was concerned. She suspected Payson felt the same way.

"I have something for you." Payson reached into a pocket and pulled out a small rag doll.

Harriet almost dropped her glass. Wine sloshed over the back of her hand and she licked it off, then set down the glass and reached for the doll. Only six inches long, the doll's white linen body had turned the color of cream, but there were no tears or holes in the fabric. She traced the finely embroidered face with a finger. The doll still had most of its pale yellow hair and wore a colorful tiered skirt and embroidered peasant blouse.

"Sunny." Harriet's voice was barely a whisper. When she looked at Payson she had tears in her eyes. Embarrassed, she looked back at the doll.

"Where did you get this?" She stroked the doll's arm with a shaking finger. "My mother made her for me." Shaking her head in wonder, she looked at him again. "I never went anywhere without this doll. I called her Sunny. She was my best friend."

"Your aunt made you leave it behind when she picked you up in Apple Valley. I'm not sure why I snagged it." He shrugged. "It felt . . . important at the time. You looked so forlorn when she made you leave it on the bench. So I took it."

Harriet hugged the doll to her. "I'm so glad you did. Memories are good, but to have tangible proof that my mother loved me . . . that's priceless."

Alex came back into the kitchen then. Harriet held the doll up for him to see.

"Payson rescued the doll my mother made me after Aunt Gwen made me leave it behind."

Understanding flared in his eyes. He got that she had nothing tangible from her parents and how precious something like the doll would be to her.

"The doll is lovely. Good for Payson." He spied the diaries on the island. "Are these the infamous diaries?"

Payson pushed them away. "Yes, but not recommended reading, I'm afraid. A disturbed piece of work, our Margaret Blackstone. She created the street drug Blitz and gave it to Mayo Sinclair to distribute. I didn't pick up a single twinge of remorse for the things she did. She killed those men, women, and children because her ego was bruised. It's almost too much to take in."

If only that were true. Because she and Payson had been personally affected by Blackstone's actions, Harriet knew they both fathomed it only too well.

"Sinclair disappeared the day the cult members died, didn't he?" Alex pulled himself a beer from the chiller. "Did you ever look for him?" As his alter ego Douglas Wade, a.k.a. the richest man on the planet, no one could hide from Payson once he put his resources and immense intelligence to work.

"I didn't. I didn't even realize he wasn't among the dead for nearly a year. He had erased and recreated himself by the time I began to search, and to be honest, I didn't care enough to pursue it." His eyes narrowed.

"Knowing what I now know about the street drug Blitz, I wish I had kept after him. At the time it didn't matter. Penny was gone and that was all I cared about."

"I know the feeling," Alex said quietly.

Harriet placed a hand on his arm and squeezed. Alex's older sister had been mugged and killed for her new trainers, a birthday present from Alex. He had blamed himself for her death and it was the main reason he had become a murder cop.

"Enough of that. Would you like to stay for supper, Payson?" Harriet asked.

His pale blue eyes twinkled. "Are you serving your famous shrimp?"

"Jeez, does everyone know about that?" Harriet felt her face heat. She was never going to live down the thoroughly charred shrimp she'd served to Alex and Solly on one of the few nights she volunteered to cook.

Alex pulled her close and kissed her temple. "Yep. Your lack of meal-making skills are infamous. I'll cook. How does pasta salad sound?"

It sounded wonderful, especially since she didn't have to make it, but Alex's link buzzed before she could answer.

"It's Fox." He opened the call. "Yeah. What's up? *What?* I'll be right there." He ended the call and shoved the link into his pants pocket.

"You'll never guess what's happened."

"Don't tell me another guest is missing." Harriet didn't think she could take any more bad news.

"All right, I won't. I will tell you that one has returned, though. Allison Beuckers just checked Patricia's room and found her sleeping in her bed. She appears to be drugged. Fox called Eleanor and she's on her way."

Eleanor Clarke, the resort's doctor, was worth her weight in gold as far as Harriet was concerned. She had saved Belle's life despite her reservations about giving a dog an antidote meant for humans.

"I'm coming with you," she said. "Belle can say here."

"Do you mind if I join you, Alex?" Payson asked.

"Not a bit. We'll take the Hog."

They arrived at the hotel at the same time as the doctor. She was dressed more casually than Harriet had ever seen her, in faded blue chinos and a tee with graphics of a long ago rock band across her chest. The five of them made their way to Patricia and Allison's first floor room.

"I didn't know who to call," Allison said, when she saw the group standing in the hall.

"You did exactly right," Tarbell told her. "This is Payson Douglas, a close friend of the resort's owner. Payson, Allison Beuckers, Patricia's companion. And this is Dr. Eleanor Clarke, the resort's doctor."

Alex, Payson, Tarbell, and Harriet waited in the sitting room of Patricia's shared suite with Allison while Eleanor examined Patricia. Her companion paced back and forth, wringing her hands.

Allison's purple beehive, so tall and impressive on the day she had reported Patricia missing, looked deflated and bedraggled. Dark shadows lay in the pockets beneath her eyes. It was obvious she cared deeply for her friend.

"Dr. Clarke knows what she's doing, Allison," Alex assured her. "If Patricia needs medical attention that we can't provide here, we'll fly her to the mainland."

"What if she's been in her room for the last two days and I never checked?" Allison Beuckers wrung her hands until her fingers turned white. "Patty could be dying because I didn't get her help soon enough."

"You had no way of knowing she would be in there," Harriet said. "What made you decide to check her room now?"

"I missed her. I went in to look at her things, to assure myself that surely she'd be back. And there she was–" she waved a hand toward the closed bedroom door. "There she was, just lying on the bed." She burst into tears.

Harriet leaped up and put her arm around the older woman's shoulders. "It's all right to cry. You've been under a tremendous strain, wondering if your friend was okay." She led Allison to one of the soft cushioned chairs.

"Sit. I'll make you a cup of tea. Or get you a glass of water. Or a drink. You need something."

She ended up making a cup of tea. Eleanor came out of the bedroom as Allison took the cup, closing the door softly behind her. Allison leaped to her feet, the cup shaking in her hand. Harriet grabbed the tea cup back before Allison spilled it.

Eleanor placed a hand on Allison's arm. "Your friend is going to be fine. She'll be hungry and desperate for a shower when she wakes from the drug she was given. I've checked her vitals. Her blood pressure is a little low, but that's to be expected with the dehydration. Her heartbeat is strong."

"Thank god." Allison collapsed in the chair. Tears streamed down her face and dripped from her chin, but she seemed oblivious to them. "I want to go home. As soon as Patty is awake, I want to go home."

"That will be arranged, Ms. Beuckers, just as soon as your friend is cleared to fly," Payson promised her. "It would be helpful if Alex and Tarbell could speak with Patricia before you leave, however. It might help us find the two women who are still missing."

"Of course. I forgot about the other women. Maybe they'll turn up the same way Patty did. Has anyone checked their beds lately?"

"We'll be sure to do that as soon as we leave here," Alex said. He turned to Eleanor. "Any idea how long Miss Williams will sleep?"

"I expect her to wake in the next hour or so. I intend to sit with her until she does." Harriet heard the words "just in case" even though Eleanor didn't speak them aloud.

Eleanor turned back toward Patricia's bedroom, but stopped to give Allison's shoulder a reassuring pat. "Your friend will be fine, I promise. I'll keep a close watch on her. If I could speak with you alone, Alex?"

Alex followed Eleanor into Patricia's bedroom and closed the door behind him.

"Something's wrong, isn't it? Otherwise why would the doctor want to talk with the security guy alone? I'm going in there."

Payson placed himself between the door and a visibly upset Allison.

"Ms. Beuckers, Dr. Clarke is not one to mince words. If she says your friend will be fine, then you can believe your friend will be fine." Payson's tone was gentle, but Harriet didn't miss the steel beneath.

"We have a serious situation here, with two missing women still out there somewhere. It may be that Dr. Clarke noticed something that will help us find them."

Before Allison could argue, the door opened and Alex came out. He held it for Allison.

"You may sit with your friend now."

Harriet waited until everyone had gathered in the hall outside the suite before rounding on Alex. "Well? What did Eleanor say?"

"She believes that Patricia was drugged with Blitz, although she won't know for sure until she gets the blood sample she took tested."

Shocked, Harriet could only stare at him. Blitz was a highly addictive street drug that induced euphoria in the user, a euphoria that blocked out everything else. Their bodies eventually gave out from lack of food and dehydration.

It was also the drug that Margaret Blackstone had developed and made for Mayo Sinclair's cult to sell. Since then, it had become a worldwide problem.

That someone on the island was using it to subdue their victims was very bad news.

CHAPTER FIFTEEN

The dim hallway was quiet but for the murmur of voices from the lobby. A woman laughed, the sound bright and happy. A door banged farther down the hallway. The scent of coconut sunscreen hung in the air.

No one spoke for a long minute.

Patricia Williams had been given Blitz. Harriet shuddered at the idea of someone shooting her body full of a drug without her consent. If someone was using Blitz to subdue women so they could kidnap them–she didn't want to think about what that would mean.

It would be so easy to do; a quick jab with a pressure syringe and a person wouldn't be able to put up a fight. They wouldn't *want* to resist. That was the whole point of the drug–it wiped out all negative feelings and transported the user to a euphoric dream land.

Anyone would be vulnerable if they were given the drug, even Alex or Tarbell.

"What makes Eleanor think Patricia was given Blitz?" Payson asked.

"I'm not sure, but she had a lot of experience with its effects when she lived on the mainland, so I trust her instincts. Something about what it does to the white's of a user's eye. It tinges them blue."

Alex fell silent when a couple with two teenaged children popped out of a suite two doors down. Laughing and chattering, they passed Harriet and the others with cheerful "G'days."

Payson's smile fell away as soon as they were out of earshot. Anger warred with disappointment in his eyes. Jaw set, he looked at Alex.

"You were right. We're going to have to introduce some new security measures on the island to protect ourselves and our guests."

Harriet knew Payson was not only disappointed in the situation, but in mankind in general. He looked as if he wanted to say more, but he gave a slight head shake.

"I'm headed home. Tag me if you learn anything more, or if the other women turn up."

Harriet watched him go and felt a sharp pang of sadness. On the surface, Payson appeared to have everything. In reality, he was a gracious and caring man who had suffered much with no one at his side to share his burdens. A lonely figure who deserved to be surrounded by a loving family. She wondered if he'd ever been married. She knew so little about his personal life. Perhaps it was time to remedy that.

Tarbell sighed and ran a hand down his face. "I'm beat."

"Go home and get some rest," Alex told him. "I'll call you if Patricia wakes up."

"What are you going to do?"

"I'm going to take Harriet back to the cottage and get some sleep myself. We need to be fresh tomorrow. Someone's playing games with us. I don't understand the rules yet, but I will. Meet me at the office at eight."

"Roger that, boss." Tarbell headed off after Payson.

"Can we leave now?" Harriet asked.

"Yes. I can't do anything more here until Patricia wakes. Eleanor will call me as soon as she's able to talk."

"Good." She took Alex's hand and led him toward the lobby, walking close to his side, seeking his warmth and the reassurance of his presence. She felt shaken up by the events of the evening, as if the ground had shifted beneath her feet.

Patricia hadn't escaped her captor; someone had returned the young woman to her bed. How had that been accomplished? Somehow that felt even more threatening than the initial kidnapping, as if the kidnapper was saying, *Look what I can do right under your noses.*

Why take Patricia in the first place if they were only going to return her two days later? Was Alex right and it was some bizarre game targeting innocent women? Even more perplexing, why play it on the resort?

What was the end game? That question bothered Harriet more than anything. There were a few common reasons why people committed murder. There were even common reasons for kidnapping; the most common being to coerce someone into doing something the kidnapper wanted.

But no one had demanded a ransom—or anything else—and yet Patricia was back in her bed. It made no sense.

Even though it wasn't that late, Venus cottage was dark when they arrived. Solly's routine had changed now that William had moved in with him. Because the pastry chef rose ultra-early to get to the kitchens, Solly now rose at the same early hour and retired early to compensate.

Harriet wished she could wake her friend. She wanted to tell him about the return of Patricia and the possible presence of Blitz in the kidnapped woman's system.

Solly felt the way she did about drugs. When they were both teens they had been part of Portland's street scene where drugs were plentiful. They had pledged to each other never to try the highly addictive Blitz and to the best of her knowledge neither had, although they'd known plenty of others who had destroyed themselves with it.

Belle came barreling out of the door as soon as Alex opened it, leaping on Harriet and knocking her back against the Hog.

"Oof. Belle. Yes, I'm happy to see you too." She rubbed the dog's ears. "I'm going to walk Belle toward the greenhouses; give her a chance to go to the bathroom. We won't be more than a few minutes."

Already halfway inside the cottage, Alex turned on his heel. "I'll come with you."

"There's no need. Really. We're only going to walk a few hundred feet and back."

Alex's gaze hardened. "I'm coming with you." He closed the door and reset the alarm.

Harriet waited for him to walk beside her. She understood his fear. At the same time, she needed him to understand that she wasn't stupid or careless. She would be careful. She didn't want him worrying about her when he needed to stay focused on the kidnapper.

"Do you think it's possible you're being a little too paranoid, Alex? What could happen to me a few hundred feet from the cottage?" When he didn't answer, she pressed.

"I'm not stupid. I know that whoever the kidnapper is, he's somehow convincing these women to go with him. I'm not going to let anyone talk me into going with them. I promise."

"I can't take the chance." Alex's tone was unyielding. "There is no one and no thing on this Earth that is more important to me than you, Twinkle Harriet Monroe. If I lost you, I would lose my reason for living."

Payson's and Alex's losses had shaped their individual lives and both men still suffered from those losses. People mourned as long as they needed to mourn. Who was she to tell them to move past the loss of a loved one? With the return of her early memories and the recently acquired knowledge of their murders, she was only beginning to truly mourn the loss of her parents.

"All right," she said quietly, and took his hand. "Thank you for caring enough to watch after me."

Alex pulled her tight to his chest. "You are everything to me." His breath felt warm and soft against her ear.

"When I'm with you, the cold and dark places inside me don't feel quite so cold or dark. I'll always hate that I lost Allysa, but when I'm with you, or thinking about you, I can forget that she was taken too soon. I can remember her laughing and the happy times, like when she tried to teach me to dance, and the good memories bring a smile now.

"You do that for me." He brushed a kiss on her temple.

Harriet took a deep breath and blinked back the tears that threatened to fall. "You do know how to sweet talk a girl," she murmured.

Alex huffed out a strangled laugh. "Let's take Belle to do her business and go to bed. I'm feeling the need to show you how much I love you."

They sauntered up the road with their arms around each other's waist and gave Belle time to sniff every bush and spot that caught her attention. The night sky sparkled with stars and the gentle breeze carried the sweet scent of night-blooming jasmine.

Harriet took it all in and felt a measure of peace that was broken by Alex's link buzzing in his pocket.

"I have to take this," he said reluctantly. He pulled it out and glanced at the screen. "It's a text from Eleanor. Patricia is awake."

Gentle, dreamy Alex was gone, replaced by the determined detective Harriet knew he'd once been and always would be.

"I'm coming with you. We have to take Belle, too. I can't leave her alone again. She hasn't been with me long enough to know I'm not abandoning her."

"Fine. Let's go." They ran back to the cottage and climbed into the Hog after loading Belle into the back. Alex handed Harriet his link.

"Tag Fox. Tell him Patricia's awake but he doesn't have to come, I'll brief him in the morning if he'd prefer to sleep." Harriet made the call.

"He's on his way," she said, tossing the link onto the seat between them.

Harriet saw the couple with the teenaged children climbing into a cart when they drove up to the hotel, most likely headed to the amusement park for some evening entertainment. It felt as if they hadn't even left. When she checked her wrist link she saw that it had only been twenty minutes since they left the hotel. And here they were again.

Tarbell jogged up to join them as they were walking down the hall to Patricia and Allison's suite. "That was fast. I'd just cracked a beer."

"Let's hope Patricia has some information for us." Alex knocked on the door. It was opened by a tearful and joyous Allison.

"She's awake! She woke up right after you left. The doctor and I got her into the shower and cleaned her up before she called you. I know Patricia wouldn't want anyone to see her in the state she was in."

The woman reminded Harriet of a mother hen clucking about her chick. Allison left them at the door and hurried back to Patricia's bedroom.

"That nice detective I was telling you about is here, Patty dear."

"Ms. Beuckers, we'd like to speak with Patricia alone if you don't mind."

It was obvious that Allison Beuckers minded very much. Her lips thinned. She fisted her hands on her hips, prepared to do battle if necessary. It was clear that no one was going to enter Patricia's room unless she was there to protect her friend.

"Allison." Harriet waited until she had the woman's attention. "Alex needs to learn what he can from Patricia so he can help the two women who are still missing. Sometimes . . . Sometimes it's difficult to speak the whole truth if someone we care about is listening because we don't want to cause them pain. It really would be best if you waited out here."

The woman seemed to crumble then. Her hands fell loosely to her sides and her shoulders slumped.

"Don't you upset her," she warned Alex, as he and Tarbell slipped past her.

"I promise to be considerate of what she's been through, Ms. Beuckers. Harriet, with me, please."

Surprised that he wanted her with him, Harriet followed Alex into the bedroom. Tarbell closed the door behind her and leaned against it, leaving Allison alone in the sitting room.

"Find a corner to observe from," Alex said in a low voice. "Don't speak unless I need your help."

Harriet picked a corner next to a low bamboo dresser and leaned against the wall. She inspected the young woman lying in the bed. Patricia looked like her photo except paler, with purple shadows beneath dull brown eyes and fresh-scrubbed skin. She had a tight grip on Eleanor's hand and plucked at the bedcover with her free hand.

Alex pulled one of the cushioned chairs next to the bed and sat. Harriet knew he was trying to appear non-threatening. Looming over Patricia from his six-four height would intimidate anyone lying flat on her back.

"Patricia, my name is Alex Hayes. I'm head of security for the resort. I used to be a detective in New York City." He smiled. "I have to admit, this is usually much more pleasant duty."

Patricia managed a small smile in return. Her grip on Eleanor relaxed slightly.

"I wonder what you can tell me about the last few days. Anything at all that you can remember. There are two other women missing and we'd very much like to have them back."

"I don't remember anything." Patricia's lower lip began to tremble.

"That's fine. No worries. What's the last thing you do remember? Let's start there."

"I woke up and I was blindfolded and gagged." Her hand tightened on Eleanor's again. "I . . . I was so afraid. Someone gave me a drink of water. I felt a pinprick on my arm. That's all I remember. Whenever I woke up they gave me a shot."

"Did the person who gave you water ever speak?"

"No." Patricia shook her head. "Yes. They wanted something."

"Good. That's really good."

Patricia looked pleased, like she'd gotten an important test answer correct.

"What did they want from you?"

Patricia was silent for so long Harriet didn't think she was going to answer.

"They needed my bank account information and passcodes."

Harriet was holding her breath. Tarbell stood still as a statue at the door. Alex leaned forward.

"That's good information, Patricia. You're doing a great job. They wanted access to your bank account. Can you tell me, did the voice belong to a man or to a woman?"

"I don't know. I gave them what they wanted and they gave me another shot." She looked at Eleanor. "Doctor, can I have a shot now?"

"Not yet. I need you to stay awake for a few more minutes. Try to answer Alex's questions, okay?"

Patricia's lips pursed in a pout. "I need another shot."

Harriet knew that Blitz was addictive, but she hadn't realized how little it took to create an addict. Eleanor would get Patricia into a rehab program, but the threat of a relapse would hang over her for the remainder of her life.

She felt her face heat with anger. No one had the right to do that to another human being. Anyone who treated another with that level of callous disregard was a monster and deserved to rot in prison until the end of their days.

She must have made a sound because everyone turned to look at her. Embarrassed, Harriet decided to address Patricia directly.

"I'm sorry for what you had to go through, Patricia, and I'm angry that someone did this to you. It was wrong. You were given a highly addictive street drug called Blitz. It makes you feel good, but it robs your vitality and it will kill you if you keep using it. There are two more women being held on this island somewhere–just like you were held. And I'm sure they're also being injected with Blitz."

Patricia was staring at her, wide-eyed. Alex was watching the woman on the bed.

"You were blindfolded so you couldn't see and gagged so you couldn't cry out for help. Could you hear anything? Smell anything? Were you inside or outdoors? Lying on a hard surface, or a soft surface like a bed?"

"I didn't hear anything. I was inside." She closed her eyes. "I was sitting on something. Kind of lying back, like on a lounger. Not hard, but firm–not squishy soft. A firm cushion, I think."

"What did you smell?" Harriet prompted.

"Myself. I stank." Her nose wrinkled. "They didn't take me to a bathroom so I had to . . you know."

"That must have been awful for you. I'm so sorry."

"And sandalwood," Patricia continued, as if Harriet hadn't spoken. "Like a really good aftershave."

"I think that's enough for now," Eleanor said as Patricia closed her eyes and sank into her pillow.

"You've been a big help. Thank you Patricia. As soon as you're able to fly we'll get you and your friend back to the mainland," Alex told her. He stood and returned the chair to its spot. Tarbell had started to pull open the door when Patricia spoke from the bed.

"Don't you want my bank information? To see if they stole all my money?"

Alex smiled. "That would be helpful. Thank you." He keyed the numbers into his link as Patricia rattled them off, thanked her again, and they left.

Harriet let Belle out when they reached the Hog. She checked to make sure no was close enough to overhear them before speaking.

"What do you think?"

"I think Patricia paid her own ransom, even though it wasn't put to her like that. They drugged her into not caring what information she gave them."

"Thanks to Harriet, Patricia gave us a few clues." Tarbell ticked them off on his fingers. "She was kept inside. Sitting on some type of lounger, not hard and not soft. And her kidnapper wears aftershave with sandalwood in it."

"So do half the male guests I've come across this week," Harriet pointed out. "Including Rodney Lynch and Martin O'Claire. I'll bet that I could walk though the hotel lobby right now and find half a dozen more men wearing sandalwood-based aftershave or cologne. It's a popular scent."

"Now what?" Tarbell looked at Alex.

"Now we go home and get some sleep. Meet me at the office

in the morning. I should have some info about Patricia's bank account by then."

They parted ways. There was very little conversation in the Hog during the drive to the cottage. Harriet climbed out of the vehicle and looked at Alex over the hood. He was staring at the ocean, deep in thought.

"A penny for them," Harriet said softly.

He looked at her, a wrinkle between his eyebrows. "Something doesn't make sense."

"What's bothering you?"

"Why bother to take Angela Daly? She's a sex worker. A highly paid one, sure, but she doesn't have the kind of dough the other two have."

Harriet held out her hand. "Perhaps she has something else the kidnapper wants. Sleep on it. I'm sure you'll find more answers in the morning."

CHAPTER SIXTEEN

Harriet found Alex in the kitchen early the following morning, drinking coffee and staring out the open lanai doors. She pressed up against his back, circling her arms around his waist.

"I see you're already in work mode. I missed our morning snuggle."

Alex pressed a hand over hers. "Me too. I woke up thinking about those poor women; tied up, blindfolded, and gagged, and shot full of dope. They must be so frightened." He turned his head to look at her, his eyes deep and blue as the North Atlantic on a sunny summer day.

"I took this job to get away from criminals. I was a fool to think the scumballs wouldn't come to the resort. They're everywhere, constantly looking for others to victimize. We're going to have to beef up the island's security force and I hate that. I hate that," he repeated quietly.

"I know." Harriet reached up and ran a finger down the scar that cut through his right eyebrow. "I have similar feelings. Poor Solly. I had a meltdown all over his shirt the other day."

She hesitated. "I'm not sure I want to work at a place the employees nickname Destination Death. But if I left, I'd feel as if I was abandoning Payson. Not to mention that I really, really love my job."

Alex turned in her arms. "That's where I'm at. Just be warned, if you decide to leave, you aren't going anywhere without me unless you tell me you no longer love me." He kissed her and pulled away.

"But for now, I have a kidnapper to find and two missing women to rescue. Are you ready to go to your office?"

fHarriet scowled at him. "I was planning to do a run this morning. I've missed too many days as it is."

"Nope. No running alone until this mess is cleared up."

"Then run with me. Solly's already left for the greenhouse so I can't ask him."

"I don't have time."

"The kidnapper isn't going to escape the island in the next hour, Alex. Besides, a run will help clear your head. You've barely thought about anything else." She didn't really think he'd agree, but it was worth a try. He surprised her when he nodded.

"Okay. You're right. It might help. Let me change and we'll go."

Harriet pumped her fist in the air when Alex left the kitchen. The man didn't stop to take care of himself when he was trying to right a wrong. Getting him to take a half hour for himself was a definite victory.

The run did them both good, as did the joint shower afterward. The furrow between Alex's brows had disappeared by the time he dropped Harriet and Belle at her office. He tossed her the key to the Hog and set off on foot for the security office after warning her to keep alert.

Harriet waited until Alex was out of sight. She had no intention of heading inside just yet. She'd had an idea that might help them identify the kidnapper—one she knew Alex wouldn't approve of—so she hadn't mentioned it.

"Come on, Belle. We have work to do." Loading Belle back into the Hog, she headed for the hotel.

Her plan was simple; walk by as many male guests as she could find and sniff. If one wore aftershave containing sandalwood, she would snap their photos–all without being noticed, of course–and then send them to Alex.

She debated leaving Belle in the Hog, but knew that Alex would be livid if he learned she'd been walking around the resort without any protection. And he would find out, since she'd have to forward him the photos of the male guests in order to identify them.

Slipping Tarbell's makeshift leash over Belle's neck, Harriet locked the Hog and headed into the hotel lobby. Two large vases filled with flowers in varying shades of purple and white offset with lacy greenery flanked the open doors. More purple and white arrangements were scattered throughout the lobby. Solly had been busy.

Harriet leaned into one of the arrangements and breathed deeply of the spicy-sweet blossoms.

"Harry! I am glad you are here. I have something for your companion."

The night clerk hurried out from behind the desk with a package wrapped in brightly colored fabric in her hand and held it out to Harriet. "This is for La Belle."

"Why are you still here?" Harriet asked. She took the package and felt it. Something round and wiggly.

Calida's bright blue eyes flashed with laughter. "You are supposed to open it, not try to guess what it is."

"Habit," Harriet admitted. "I get so few gifts that I try to draw out the suspense." She untied the raffia holding the fabric. A braided, dark brown leather leash with a loop in one end and a brass snap on the other lay coiled inside.

"Oh, it's a dog leash! How did you know I needed one? It's

beautiful, Calida. Thank you." She threw her arms around the girl and hugged her.

"I see the piece of rope Fox rigged for the dog and I think such a beautiful beast deserves much better. You like it? I made it."

"You didn't. Really?" Harriet inspected the precisely plaited, thin leather strips. "Wow. I'm really impressed. I've never seen such a beautiful leash." She hooked the brass snap onto the ring on Belle's collar and removed the lead Tarbell had rigged for her and stuffed it into her bag.

"You could easily sell these."

Calida shrugged but looked pleased. "Perhaps. I must go now. Antonio is waiting for me. We are going to have breakfast together."

She indicated a handsome man standing outside the lobby near the benches in front of the hotel, watching them. Harriet recognized him as one of the baggage clerks who worked with her friend Albie.

"Ah, I see," Harriet said, with a smile and a wink. "Have a wonderful breakfast with your friend. And thank you again. The leash is one of the nicest gifts I've ever received. I'm blown away that you made it. Belle looks more regal with it on, don't you agree?"

Calida ruffled the dog's ears and kissed her between the eyes. "Beautiful Belle. We take good care of you, eh? Bye, Harry."

From the wide smile on Antonio's face, Harriet guessed the couple were more than just friends. She watched him wrap his arm around Calida's shoulders and pull her close. She felt happy for Calida. Working for the resort meant isolation from the mainland for weeks on end, a difficult situation for the single employees.

Harriet wandered the lobby in a slow, haphazard manner, stopping near the male guests to sniff the air. Rodney Lynch–

Fitness Guy–passed by without acknowledging her, leaving a trail of sandalwood in his wake.

By the time she finished her circuit of the lobby, she had taken seven photos of men wearing sandalwood-based aftershave that morning. Unfortunately, she'd only seen a small handful of the hotel's guests in the lobby. What about the ones staying in the cottages? How many male guests were on the island?

She was beginning to understand that maybe her bright idea hadn't been too bright after all. Who knew that sandalwood would prove to be so popular? She was beginning to think that most men who wore aftershave smelled of sandalwood. It would be easier to eliminate the men who were *not* wearing the popular fragrance.

"Good morning, Miss Monroe. I've been trying to guess what you're up to, but I'm afraid your actions elude me."

Martin O'Claire smiled down at her, humor dancing in his unusual eyes. Harriet swallowed back a groan. Apparently she hadn't been as nonchalant as she'd thought in her search for men wearing sandalwood aftershave. How many others had seen her and questioned her behavior? She hoped none of them thought they should report the strange woman with the dog.

She sniffed the air. Even O'Claire wore sandalwood.

He narrowed his eyes and gave her a speculative look. "Did you just smell me? Are you looking for something special?"

Only a kidnapper who keeps his victims drugged until they agree to give him their money.

"Oh. No. I was just conducting an informal survey. Nothing important. Gosh, look at the time. I really need to be getting to my office. Enjoy your day, Mr. O'Claire."

Harriet knew she was being rude, especially when O'Claire had been nothing but nice and polite towards her, but the truth was, until they identified the kidnapper she didn't trust anyone who wasn't a co-worker. She made a beeline for the doors, loaded Belle into the Hog, and drove away from the hotel before anyone else tried to speak with her.

Because Alex expected her to be in her office, she parked out front, but then hesitated to go inside. She sat in the Hog and drummed her fingers on the steering wheel while she tried to sort her jumbled thoughts. She wished her parents were alive so she could ask them for guidance, but visiting their graves was the closest she would ever come to being with them.

Fifteen minutes later, she found herself parking the Hog at Payson's cottage. There was no answer when she knocked on the door and the cottage was locked.

"He told me I could visit the graves whenever I wanted," she told Belle. "Payson never says anything he doesn't mean. Come on, let's go see my parents."

Harriet led Belle around the cottage to the rear. Despite knowing its approximate location, it took her several minutes to find the well hidden, narrow path in the thick growth. Once she set foot on it, however, it was easy to follow.

She pushed aside gnarly vines and large, shiny leaves, careful not to bruise them, unlike the day Payson had showed her the graves, when her mind had things other than hiking through the jungle. Things like why he had been so keen to hire her.

Living with her aunt and uncle, and then in the city after she'd run away, she hadn't had many opportunities to hike in the countryside—but she'd learned a few things about nature since moving to the island.

She'd learned that everything that lived or grew or flew on the island had a right to be there, and she needed to minimize her impact on any of them. If Payson could travel the path to the family graveyard and leave very little sign, then she would honor that and do her best to follow suit.

Focused on the plants that crowded the trail, she almost missed the sun's rays lighting a large spider web strung across the trail. It took her a minute to locate its builder: a black and brown spider the size of her palm, lying in wait on the web's upper right edge.

"Ew." Suppressing a shudder, Harriet ducked beneath the web. Just because a creature had a right to its life didn't mean she had to embrace it. Unlike her mother, spiders frightened her.

The trail ended abruptly, and sooner than she expected. Belle pulled her free of the thick jungle and bounded across the bed of blue flowers toward a figure sitting cross-legged in front of Penelope's grave marker.

Dismayed, Harriet stopped. "I'm sorry, Payson. It didn't occur to me that you might be here." She turned back to the trail. "I'll come back later."

"No. Please stay. You're welcome here anytime."

Harriet hesitated, unsure if he meant it or was just being polite. Payson sensed her indecision and smiled.

"I mean it. Please stay. I find this spot a good place for quiet contemplation."

"Thank you." She stepped forward and dropped to her knees in front of her mother's grave marker.

"I was feeling out of sorts. I couldn't concentrate on work and Alex doesn't want me to go anywhere unescorted until our kidnapper is caught. My brain is being pulled in so many directions . . . I feel a mess, frankly."

"It happens to the best of us, Harry, and you've had a particularly difficult stretch. Would it help to talk about it?"

Harriet traced her mother's name on the stone. "Alex asked me to marry him."

"Is that a problem? I think you and Alex make a fine couple."

"No, it's not a problem. I definitely want to marry him. It's just . . . I told him I wasn't ready. It's because I feel such a mess. My memories have barely begun to return. I might be a little worried about what I'm going to learn about myself."

Payson raised an eyebrow but said nothing.

"What if I'm not a nice person? What if I turn out to be selfish and self-centered?"

"That's hardly likely," Payson said dryly. "The essence of your personality has always been with you, regardless of what you remember from your childhood."

Harriet gestured toward Belle. "What was I thinking, bringing her here? I have a responsibility to look after Belle and I don't know the first thing about dogs. What kind of training should we do together? How much exercise does she need? Am I feeding her the proper foods? I took away her opportunity to be adopted by someone who knows what they're doing when I didn't take her to the animal shelter like I should have. Did I do her a disservice?

"And if I'm this befuddled when it comes to caring for a pet what sort of mother will I make? I have no one to run to when I have questions and Alex is no better off." She knew she sounded crazy. She hadn't even realized that she was worried about becoming a mother until the words popped out.

Payson laughed and shook his head. "Those are good questions. I believe the fact that you are asking them shows that you are aware of the pitfalls. Sometimes awareness is all we have. I've learned that when I know I need answers they somehow find their way to me. I've only known you a short while, Harry, but I believe you will make an excellent mother."

They sat in silence for several minutes while Harriet digested Payson's words. The sound of the waves quietly lapping the rocky shore began to work their magic. She felt her shoulders begin to relax. Lord, she'd been tense lately.

"Anything else on your mind?"

Now that she'd begun, she found it easy to rattle off the things that were bothering her.

"Solly's boyfriend and new roommate William is hiding something and I'm worried for Solly."

"William our pastry chef? What makes you think he's hiding something?"

"I overheard his side of a link conversation outside the kitchens one day. He was upset–angry upset–but when I asked him if there was anything I could do to help, he denied there was anything wrong. Only that's a lie. Someone wants something from him and he was telling whoever was on the other end of the link that he needed more time."

"I know how much Solomon means to you, but I think you'll have to let that one sort itself out. It will, in time. Is there more?"

Harriet didn't want to speak the more. She didn't want to hurt the man who'd become important to her, a favorite uncle without the blood ties. Maybe even a father figure, if she was being honest. She looked into Payson's calm blue eyes and knew she needed to be honest or forever hold her peace.

"I'm unhappy with the way things are going here on the island. Have you heard the employees have nicknamed the resort Destination Death?"

Payson nodded. "They're not wrong. The number of deaths has been unexpected and disheartening."

"It's awful. You built something wonderful here, but it's being spoiled–taken over–by a few inconsiderate creeps. And now this latest creep is kidnapping guests and drugging them until they agree to pay their own ransom. It's . . ."

She shook her head, hating to say the words. Looking out at the beautiful turquoise water rather than watching his face, she spoke in a near whisper.

"I love my job, Payson, I really do. But I don't love this aspect of it. It's getting to be too much."

"I agree."

Surprised, Harriet jerked around to look at him. "You do?"

"I've been having the same thoughts." He indicated his sister's grave. "I came here to talk to Penny about them. She can't answer me back, but I can guess what she would say. I find it helps."

"Yeah." Harriet recalled her thoughts when Payson had left them outside Patricia's suite; how lonely he looked.

"Payson, have you ever been married?"

"Once. A lifetime ago. It didn't stick. I went off the rails for a while after Penny's death, thinking I'd failed my little sister. I eventually drove my wife away."

"What was she like–your wife?"

"Stella?" He thought for a minute. "She was my anchor. She kept my feet on the ground when the money really began to roll in. She reminded me every day about what was important; that money was only a means to an end, not an end itself. She was beautiful and I loved her dearly. I almost didn't survive her leaving."

"I'm sorry," Harriet said softly. "Did she remarry?"

Payson looked uncomfortable. "No. At least not the last time I checked."

"So you . . . still keep track of her." Was she treading on tabooed ground?

"Off and on." He rose to his feet in one smooth move, still agile despite his sixty-plus years. A middle-aged man who took good care of his body.

But what about his heart?

"You likely have decades ahead of you, Payson," Harriet pointed out. "Do you plan to spend them alone?"

"I have a holo business meeting to attend in twenty minutes. I need to get changed." He left without answering her question.

Harriet sat in the sun and the quiet, smelling the flowers' perfume, listening to the sea and the birds and the quiet rustle of leaves in the soft breeze until she knew what she had to do.

CHAPTER SEVENTEEN

The visit to her parents' graves left a variety of emotions churning inside Harriet. She'd been surprised to learn that Payson felt as disappointed as she did with the way certain guests treated the island as their hunting ground. Unfortunately, she didn't see how he could stop it, even if they started screening the guests before they arrived.

It was sad but true that people who intended to do harm would always find a way to achieve their goal.

Alex called before Harriet made it back to her office. She felt a twinge of guilt that she hadn't told him about her parents' graves yet. Worse, she wasn't sure *why* she hadn't told him. Was it because the knowledge was still so fresh and new that she was still absorbing it? Whatever the reason, she suspected he'd be hurt when he found out she'd kept the discovery to herself.

Her link buzzed again. She hesitated to answer until she realized he'd be frantic if he couldn't reach her.

"Alex. What's up?"

"Where are you? I checked the office and you aren't there."

"I'm headed there now. I wanted to speak with Payson about something. What's happened?"

"Azzi DeBerry is back. Someone found her sleeping on a bench in front of the hotel. Eleanor is checking her over now."

Harriet didn't wait for an invitation. "I'm on my way. I just passed the spa road. I should be there in five."

It felt like déjà vu when Tarbell let her into Azzi's suite. Eleanor was in Azzi's bedroom with the young woman. Alex and Tarbell sat with Krystina in the sitting room, waiting to speak with the kidnap victim.

Unlike Patricia's protective companion, Azzi's roommate Krystina–"that's with a K and a Y," she informed Harriet–gulped down a large glass of wine and poured another, all while giving Tarbell flirty glances.

"Nice leash," Tarbell said, fingering the plaited leather.

"Calida made it."

"That girl has some serious skills. She'd have no problem selling those on the mainland."

Eleanor opened Azzi's bedroom door before Harriet could reply.

"How is she?" Alex asked.

"Same as Patricia." Eleanor tucked her stethoscope into her jacket pocket. "She's dehydrated and drugged. Patricia's blood sample showed Blitz in her system. I'm confident in saying that the kidnapper used it on Azzi, and probably Angela Daly, as well. Unlike Patricia, Azzi is awake. Her last dose must have been a while ago. You may speak with her now, if you like."

"Fox. Harriet." Alex jerked his head toward the bedroom door. Eleanor returned to Azzi's bedside and took her hand. Alex dragged a chair opposite the doctor and sat. Wanting to stay out of the way but still be able to hear and see, Harriet leaned against the wall next to the door with Belle at her side. Tarbell stood next to her, his attention focused on the woman in the bed.

Azzi didn't look quite as beaten down from her ordeal as Patricia had. Her long blonde hair hung in greasy lanks and her lips were dry and cracked, but her sea green eyes held a spark that Patricia's had lacked.

"Azzi, this is Alex Hayes, the security manager for the resort." Eleanor spoke softly while she gently pressed the woman's wrist beneath her fingers. The doctor was monitoring her pulse, Harriet realized. "He'd like to ask you a few questions if you're up for it."

Azzi gave Alex a long, considering look.

"I'm definitely up for it." Her voice sounded raspy. Eleanor held a glass of water to her lips.

"Drink. You're dehydrated." Azzi took a long sipped and thanked her.

"Bastard took my money. He better have left me some."

Harriet felt Tarbell stiffen next to her like a bird dog who'd just located its prey. It wasn't hard to guess why. Azzi had been in the kidnapper's possession for less time than Patricia, and even though she looked awful, she sounded far more lucid. With any luck she'd be able to provide details that would help them find the kidnapper.

"What can you tell us about him? Or where he held you?" Alex asked. "Anything, even the smallest detail, could help us."

"He wore sandalwood aftershave and never spoke. At least, he never spoke until he told me he'd let me go if I agreed to pay a ransom." She frowned and looked off, clearly thinking back.

"I think he used one of those gadgets that distorts your voice."

Alex exchanged a glance with Tarbell, their excitement palpable.

"Start from the beginning," Alex urged. "He took you from your bed. Do you remember him entering your bedroom?"

Azzi shook her head. "No. When I woke up I was blindfolded and gagged and trussed up like an over-wrapped package. I couldn't move, couldn't shout for help."

Harriet saw the pulse in Azzi's neck beat faster at the

memory. Eleanor stroked her arm and made soothing noises. After several deep breaths and another sip of water, Azzi continued.

"Krystina and I were partying with two guys from Nebraska. I was pretty wasted. At first I thought maybe I'd gone back to their room and things had gotten out of hand, but as soon as someone shot me full of dope I knew they weren't involved."

"How could you be so sure?" Harriet asked. "The guys from Nebraska could have tied you up and given you drugs."

Azzi shook her head. "Not them. They're so clean, they squeak." She gave a wry smile. "I would know. I started using after my mother died. If it wasn't for Krissy getting me into a rehab, I'd be dead by now." She looked at Alex.

"There's something about users and dealers that other users and dealers can sense, you know? It's like you can smell the drugs on them. Feel it in their auras or something. The Nebraska boys are clean. And they don't wear sandalwood, their aftershave is more musky." She smiled at Alex's puzzled look.

"I used to work the fragrance counter at Vanity." She dropped her head back onto the pillows stacked behind her and closed her eyes. Eleanor gave Alex a warning look. He gave a quick nod back, acknowledging the need to wrap it up.

"Did the kidnapper keep you drugged, Azzi?"

"Yep." She answered without opening her eyes. "I'm jonesing for a another hit right now. I'm going to have to go into rehab again. Bastard."

"Dr. Clarke will give you something to help as soon as we finish. I'll need your bank info so I can try to trace the money. Can you think of anything else that might help me identify the kidnapper?"

Azzi remained quiet for so long that Harriet thought she'd fallen asleep. She spoke without opening her eyes.

"He only talked that one time and it was in a whisper and

distorted-like. He sounded educated, but then anyone who can afford to come here would be, wouldn't they? He moved me once. I was lying in a bed when I first woke up and he moved me to a lounger. He was strong, but I could tell he wasn't a big man, you know? Not like Gary."

Gary? Puzzled, Harriet looked at Tarbell.

"One of the Nebraska brothers," he whispered in her ear.

"Azzi needs to get cleaned up now and sleep," Eleanor said. "Azzi, I'm going to send Krystina in. We'll help you shower and get into some clean clothes."

Harriet and Tarbell left the room while Alex lingered to get the bank information. He joined them in the hallway outside the suite moments later.

"Let's find somewhere more private to talk."

They ended up at the employee canteen. Because of the odd hour, the place was only one third full and they were able to snag their usual back corner table on the outside patio. All three ordered a full breakfast with a shared pitcher of fresh-squeezed orange juice.

No one spoke until their meals had been delivered and mostly consumed. The sweet, citrusy juice helped dissipate some of the bitterness left in Harriet's mouth after hearing Azzi recount her kidnapping.

"So." Alex pushed away his empty plate. "According to Azzi, our kidnapper is strong, but not a "big" man." He made air quotes around big. "I've interviewed Gary and Daniel Whitfield, a.k.a. the Nebraska brothers. They're about six-two and broad in the shoulder, so I'm going to go out on a limb and say the man we're looking for is around six foot and in excellent physical condition, but not bulky."

"He's also educated and persuasive," Tarbell added. "Don't forget he talked Patricia Williams into leaving the hotel lobby with him."

"And he wears sandalwood aftershave. Both women mentioned that," Harriet pointed out. Alex took the last piece of chocolate filled croissant off her plate and popped it into his mouth.

"Hey! I was going to eat that."

She was going to have to train him not to eat from her plate or there were going to be some heated battles in their future. He winked at her, and it occurred to her that he took food from her plate just to wind her up.

She shook her head in exasperation. Being loved by Alex was going to keep her on her toes, but finding ways to repay him for winding her up could be fun. It would certainly make for an interesting marriage.

If she ever got her head straight and asked him. She pushed away the thought and focused on the kidnapper. Did they have enough information to start narrowing the field of suspects?

"What's next?" Tarbell asked. He poured the last of the juice into his glass and downed it.

"We start with splitting the list of male guests and interviewing them all. Cross them off the list if they don't look strong enough to lift a woman, or if they wear an aftershave that doesn't smell of sandalwood. Then we'll combine the names that are left and dig deeper."

"Does that mean you're convinced the kidnapper isn't a male employee of the resort?"

Tarbell had asked a good question. Harriet waited to hear how Alex would respond.

"No, I'm not convinced of anything at this point."

"It would be easier for an employee to know where to stash the women," Tarbell said. "That's all I'm saying. I don't think we should exclude them."

"Noted. I'll include them on the list."

"What about me? How can I help?"

"You can help by heading to your office and staying there."

"All right." She smirked inwardly when she saw the surprise in Alex's eyes. She knew he had expected her to argue, but she had something important to do and her office was as good a place as any.

She stood and pushed her chair in. "Tag me if anything changes or Angela Daly shows up. I'll be in my office."

CHAPTER EIGHTEEN

Although Harriet did intend to go to her office, there was something she needed to do first. She pulled out her link and shot Alex a text, letting him know she was making a stop at the greenhouses before she went to her office. There was a time not that long ago when she would have resented having to report her plans to him, but now she considered it a sign of how much they'd grown to care for one another.

Keeping each other informed of what they were up to was what happily married couples did. She wasn't sure how or when she'd come by that belief, but there it was. If you loved someone you didn't make them worry needlessly.

And she did love him.

So why was she shying away from marriage?

The main buildings of the resort and the guests dropped away as she followed the shell road south. She rolled down the Hog's front windows to let in the lovely air. Apparently she wasn't the only one who enjoyed the smell of salt water mixed with lush jungle; Belle immediately stuck her head out and shut her eyes. Her ears and loose lips flapped in the breeze, making Harriet laugh.

Not for the first time, she wondered about Belle's age and breeding. She'd have to read Margaret Blackstone's diaries more carefully to see if the chemist mentioned acquiring Belle. Maybe she could post a photo on a few dog sites to see if anyone there could help her identify Belle's breed.

She checked the time when she approached the cottages and realized that with his new hours Solly could already be home from work. Wheeling the Hog behind Venus Cottage, she hopped out and held the door for Belle.

"Come on, sweetie. Let's see if our neighbor is home yet." Belle leaped from the Hog and immediately began to sniff the ground around Venus's back door.

With luck, William would still be working and she'd have her friend all to herself. It was selfish of her, but she missed seeing Solly every day. He was the brother she'd never had. The one person on the planet who knew her almost as well as she knew herself. He was her family. It was good that her friend had someone special in his life, but did that have to mean that she was no longer a part of it?

She was halfway around the side of the cottage when raised voices caught her attention. She stopped and grabbed Belle's collar. If Solly and William were arguing, she did not want to get in the middle of a lover's spat.

She backed away, intent on returning to the Hog before anyone noticed her, when she realized William wasn't arguing with Solly; he was arguing with Martin O'Claire. Why would William be arguing with the preacher? Harriet stilled and cupped her free hand behind her ear.

"You owe me." She shivered at the threat in O'Claire's deep, smooth voice.

"I owe you nothing." William's voice trembled, belying the brave words.

"Don't forget—you have this job because of me, and I can just as easily see it taken away and see that you never find another position as a pastry chef."

"You wouldn't. I know too much."

Harriet didn't want to hear any more. Pulling Belle with her, she slowly backed away and returned to the Hog. Grateful for the silent, hydrogen-powered engine, she started it up and continued down the road toward the greenhouses. She parked two minutes later, still unsettled by the conversation between William and O'Claire.

Solly sat at his office desk when she found him, so engrossed in filling out a ledger that he didn't notice her standing in the doorway. She took advantage of the unusual opportunity to observe him, noting the gold sun streaks in his hair and his relaxed posture. He'd always been a beautiful man, but since coming to the island he had grown even more so.

Rejected by a father who refused to accept that his son preferred men over women, Solly had always been comfortable in his own skin. It was one of the things that had drawn her to him—that, and his supreme confidence that he could achieve anything he went after. Case in point, he'd always wanted a job in horticulture—but not just any job—he wanted to manage, and one day own, his own greenhouses.

He made a great leap toward achieving that when he took the position as head gardener for the Island Resort. She held no doubts that he would own his own greenhouses when he left his current position—if that was still his dream. Solly had the perfect set-up on the island with none of the financial risk owning his own business would bring, and he was wise enough to realize it.

"Are you going to stand there staring at me all afternoon or are you here for a reason?"

Harriet grinned and moved into the office, taking a chair from the stack against the wall and setting it in front of the desk.

"I didn't think you knew I was here. You seemed totally absorbed in your ledger thing."

"I heard Belle's nails on the slate." He dated his ledger entry and signed with a flourish before snapping it shut and leaning back in his chair.

"Something good?" Harriet nodded toward the ledger. "You seemed happy about it."

"Progress in my hybridization program. I'm not there yet, but I can smell success."

"That's great, Sol. I'm proud of you. Soon they'll be calling you the new Lucifer Burbank."

"Luther, not Lucifer. Don't malign the name of my horticultural hero. What brings you to my neck of the island? Any news on our kidnapper?"

"The second victim, Azzi DeBeery, was found this morning sleeping on a bench in front of the hotel. She'd been drugged with Blitz, just like Patricia Williams."

"Was she able to tell Alex anything useful?"

"Not really, no, other than our kidnapper wears sandalwood aftershave, uses a distorter to disguise his voice, and is not as big and powerful as Gary Whitfield."

Solly blinked. "All right. I'll bite. Who the hell is Gary Whitfield?"

"One of two brothers from Nebraska who are here on the island to celebrate some big deal they recently closed." Harriet shrugged. "That's basically all I know except that Azzi is hoping to see more of brother Gary from Nebraska."

"And that helps Alex how?"

"It doesn't. Just like with Patricia, the kidnapper released Azzi after she shared her bank information with him. Alex is trying to track her money and he and Tarbell are interviewing the male guests and employees. Three women kidnapped, two returned, and he's no closer to identifying the culprit."

"He must be frustrated."

"He is," Harriet agreed. She picked at a cuticle and frowned. It used to be so easy to talk with Solly about anything. She hadn't expected to feel uncomfortable.

"Spit it out. I can see something's on your mind." He knew her so well. The knowledge dispelled her discomfort.

"Alex asked me to marry him."

"He did? That's great–isn't it? I know you love him."

"I do. I do love him. But I said no."

"What? Are you nuts? You won't find a more solid, truer mate than Alex Hayes."

"I know." Unable to sit still, Harriet rose and began to pace the small office.

"It's not him I'm worried about. It's me."

"I don't understand." Solly's warm brown eyes followed her.

"I don't completely understand myself; but now that my memories are returning and I'm learning things about my past I– I'm not entirely sure who I am any more. What if deep down I'm not ready to settle with one man? I had a fierce crush on Mark. I even asked him to sleep with me."

Solly's eyebrows shot to his hairline.

"You're kidding. I knew you were attracted to him but–asking him to sleep with you? That's so uncharacteristic."

"It was when we were searching the east cabins and got stuck there overnight. I had too much to drink. Mark refused, of course, and we moved past it. And I didn't tell you because I was embarrassed."

"Do you still want to sleep with him?"

"No." Harriet placed her hands on the desk and leaned forward.

"Mark isn't the point. What if it happens again? Maybe I'm really a-a loose woman at heart. Maybe I'll want to have sex with every attractive man I spend time with."

Solly laughed. He shook his head. "Harry, you are one of the least promiscuous women I know. You have nothing to worry about. Trust me."

"What about Mark? I really wanted to get naked with him."

"Only because you were drunk at the time. If you'd been sober you never would have propositioned him. To be honest, my estimation of the man has shot up knowing he turned you down. Being attracted to others is natural. It's what we do with it that counts."

Harriet still didn't feel convinced.

"All right, answer me this. How many men have you wanted to have sex with—ever? All time?"

"Three," Harriet answered promptly. "My ex, Alex, and Mark. Four. Simon."

"Simon? Long-haired, lanky Simon from the streets? You were seventeen and he was what? Twenty-seven?"

"I found him attractive. He had a beautiful face."

"Never mind. He doesn't count. How many attractive men have you met in that time?"

Harriet shrugged. "I couldn't begin to even count." She saw what he was getting at and plopped back into the chair.

"Too much has happened in too short a space of time. My brain is overflowing. I don't know who I am any more."

"You'll figure it out. You're still you, Harry; there's just more of you that needs time to integrate. And it's been an exceptionally rough week. It's no wonder your emotions are all over the place. How did Alex respond when you refused his offer?"

"He said he wouldn't ask again. I have to ask him."

"That's all right, then. You've known each other less than a year. It wouldn't hurt to wait a few more months, maybe even a full year. Just to make sure there are no surprises."

"Alex is the most straight forward person I've ever met, Sol. He's even more forthright than you. What I see is what I'll get.

There will be no surprises. He's nothing like my ex, Bradley. He doesn't play games." Bradley Higgins had been a colossal mistake that had cost her her female friends and almost destroyed her friendship with Solly.

"It sounds as if you want to marry him."

"I do."

"Then why are we having this conversation?"

Did he really not see how they'd drifted apart? Harriet ran her fingers through her hair and tugged.

"It feels like we don't get to talk any more. We used to run together every morning, but now you're already gone when I get up. We have dinner together once in a while instead of nearly every night–but never just the two of us so we can really talk–"

"You can't talk with William there? Why not?"

"Because I don't know William. And so far he has resisted all my efforts to remedy that fact. Frankly, I don't think he likes me very much, although how he can pass judgement without spending more time with me . . ." She threw her hands up in the air.

"Here's the truth. There's something hinky about your boyfriend, Sol. He's hiding something and it makes me nervous because I have no idea what it could be and I'm afraid you're going to get hurt."

They glared at each other for several long moments. Belle lay at Harriet's feet and whined, a worried, almost human expression on her face. Harriet leaned down to rub the dog's ears and reassure her.

"Sorry, Belle. Neither of us is angry with you."

"I stopped by Venus Cottage on my way here in case you'd already gone home," she added, keeping her gaze on Belle instead of Solly. "I heard William arguing with the preacher Martin O'Claire. They sounded as if they knew each other. Remember a couple nights ago when we thought William was having a panic attack? It happened when O'Claire joined us on your lanai. There's something going on between William and the preacher. "

When Solly didn't respond, she looked up, only to find her friend staring at her with a look of disbelief on his face.

"I can't believe you resent me having someone in my life."

Confusion and sadness washed over Harriet. She and Solly were usually on the same wave length. Of all the things Solly could have said, that was not the response she'd expected. How could he believe she wasn't happy for him? She felt hot tears prick at her eyes and blinked them back. She would not cry.

"How can you think that? I'm happy for you, Sol. I really am. I've been waiting for you to find someone you want to keep around for longer than a month. But William is hiding something. I know it. And you do too, only you won't admit it."

A wave of tiredness washed over Harriet. The last thing she wanted to do was argue with the man who used to be her closest friend. She stood and replaced the chair.

"I have to go. I told Alex I'd be at the office if he needs me." She turned and left Solly's office without saying goodbye, loaded Belle into the Hog, and headed back to the main resort, fighting back tears all the way.

CHAPTER NINETEEN

Harriet replayed her conversation with Solly over and over again while she drove to her office; yet no matter how she looked at it, she still felt angry and confused by the clear disconnect that had cropped up between them. She felt as if she'd unexpectedly lost a limb–some essential piece of her was missing, and it frightened her to think she might never get it back.

She and Solly never fought. They barely even argued; not one truly serious disagreement in all the years they'd been best friends and roommates. The only other time things had been tense between them was when Solly tried to warn her that her fiancé at the time was slowly taking control of her life by cutting her off from her friends. She hadn't been able to see it and she had dismissed his concerns. Eventually Solly had been proven right.

She dashed a few tears from her cheeks and took a deep breath. Maybe she'd been too hasty to walk out when Solly accused her of not wanting him to have someone special in his life. On the other hand, how could he believe that she would want him to be alone for the rest of his life? She had always supported and only wanted the best for him, and she knew how much he cared for William. Why couldn't he see that she was only looking out for him?

Because Solly was in the middle of it, just like she'd been when she couldn't see how Bradley had manipulated her.

"Crap. I'm an idiot."

Belle pulled her head in the window and looked at Harriet.

"Nothing to do with you, pretty girl. Just a little trouble on the home front."

There was no sign of either William or Martin O'Claire when Harriet passed the cottages. She watched the beach for the preacher's distinctive form as she drove, but didn't see him. What could she do if she did see him? Asking him about a private conversation between him and William would be rude. Whatever was going on with the two men was really none of her business.

She wished she'd never said anything to Solly. He was happy with William. Who was she to interfere?

Her link buzzed as she approached the main resort. Hoping it was Solly calling to apologize, she answered it without checking caller I.D.

"Harry. Payson Douglas called me a half hour ago. He wants to set up separate meetings with the employees of each department tomorrow morning. Do you happen to know what it's all about?"

"Cassie." Harriet fought to keep the disappointment from her voice. She had really hoped to hear from Solly.

"Obviously. Now tell me, what do you know?"

"Payson wants to meet with the resort employees?" Harriet frowned. "I have no idea why."

"Shoot. I thought since you two seem to have a special relationship that he'd have shared. Since Payson is Wade's mouthpiece I'm hoping the big man isn't going to pull the plug on the resort after everything that's happened, you know?"

Sometimes Harriet wished she didn't know that Payson

Douglas and Douglas Wade were the same man. She had to remind herself when talking with others that Payson was Wade's secret identity and be careful not to let anything slip that might let the secret out.

"I don't think you have to worry about Wade closing the resort, Cass." Harriet pictured Payson's private cemetery and knew he would never leave his sister's grave behind. "Maybe he wants to do some restructuring. Or just wants some feedback on how things are going and suggestions for improvement. You know how those corporate types are–always looking for more data."

"Watch it. I'm one of those corporate types, you know."

Harriet smirked at her friend. "And you're so good at it." It was true. Cassie juggled a lot of balls and kept the resort running smoothly–other than the occasional murder and kidnappings–but they weren't Cassie's fault.

"When do you want me to meet with Mr. Douglas? I can be available any time, or sit in with one of the other groups if you'd prefer."

"He requested that he see you last, at eleven. I'll be sitting in on each of the meetings except yours. Let's hope you're right and he won't be giving us all pink slips." Cassie scowled and cut the call.

"Well." Harriet drummed her fingers on the steering wheel. "I wonder what Payson is up to, Belle. Did he happen to tell you anything when we saw him? No? I didn't think so."

Belle cocked her head as if she was trying to understand what Harriet was saying, nudged Harriet's hand for a few pets, then returned to monitoring the passing scenery outside the window.

Harriet slowed to a crawl and maneuvered the Hog around a couple of women carrying towels and drinks, obviously headed to the beach. Her link was still in her hand when it buzzed again.

"Sol?"

"No, it's me. Where are you?"

"Almost to the office. Why?" The tension in Alex's voice fairly crackled through the link. "Alex, what's wrong?"

"I need you to go to the spa and pick up Eleanor. Meet me at the shuttle pad."

"What's wrong? Who's hurt?" If Alex needed Eleanor to meet him at the shuttle pad, that meant someone was seriously hurt and needed to be flown to the mainland.

"Get here quick as you can, Harriet. Gotta go." He cut the call without answering her question.

"Belle, pull your head in." Harriet waited for the dog to comply and put the window up enough so she couldn't stick her head back out. Belle gave her a disappointed look and wedged her nose in the crack.

"Sorry, girl. I don't want you to get hit in the eye." She waited for several people to cross the road in front of the hotel, then drove as fast as she dared, passing the slower carts she encountered with a warning beep.

Set on the first cove, it only took Harriet five minutes to reach the spa road once she was out of the hotel traffic. She turned off the main shell road at the yellow limestone marker that read simply "Spa" and was forced to drive more slowly. Despite the fact that workers cleared back the growth on an almost daily schedule, the jungle was relentless in its effort to overtake the resort's roads.

Apparently the spa road hadn't been cleared recently. Sunbeams pierced the trees that met overhead, flecking the road with light and shadow that screwed with her depth perception. Broad green leaves brushed against the vehicle's side.

A heavy vine slapped against the edge of the Hog's windshield and hit the end of Belle's nose. She pulled back and gave Harriet an indignant look.

"I told you," Harriet muttered. She veered from the right side where she'd been traveling in case a guest came from the opposite direction, into the center of the road and arrived at the spa without further incident.

The doctor was waiting with her bag in front of the low, pale stone building. She hurried toward Harriet as Harriet circled the Hog around the large clump of tall, furry-leaved Angel's Trumpets that filled the center of the circular drive.

The heavy, sweet scent of the over-sized, trumpet-shaped flowers hung on the air. A sign had been placed in front of the pale peach-colored blossoms since her last visit to the spa.

"Warning. Poisonous. Do Not Touch."

Harriet jumped out of the Hog and moved Belle into the back.

"Did we have a problem?" she asked, indicating the sign as Eleanor climbed into the vehicle.

"Just being careful. A few of the guests were showing a little too much interest."

The Angel's Trumpets were a source of scopolamine, a drug used in small amounts for motion sickness and nausea, but if too much was taken it caused hallucinations and temporary paralysis. Some people would think nothing of ingesting the plant in their search for a "high" or out-of-body experience.

"Let's go. Time is of the essence."

Harriet climbed behind the wheel and started the engine. "What's happening at the shuttle pad? Alex didn't tell me anything when he asked me to pick you up. I thought the pad was deserted except during arrivals and departures."

She headed back down the center of the spa road, keeping a sharp eye for guests in carts heading in to the spa.

"Oh, no." Letting her foot up on the accelerator, Harriet glanced at her passenger. "Don't tell me it's one of the kidnapped women. What's happened? Did Azzi or Patricia have a drug reaction?"

"Harriet." Eleanor didn't bother to hide her exasperation.

"What? It must be something terrible or you would tell me."

"Just drive. The sooner we get there the sooner you'll find out what's going on."

"Right." Harriet pressed on the accelerator and the Hog shot forward. They passed the pirate coves and the marina going as fast as Harriet had ever driven. She tightened her grip on the wheel and sent up a quick prayer when the Hog's back end skidded as they made the turn into the shuttle pad.

Three turquoise and white planes, all marked with a stylized WD on the tail fin, gleamed in the center of the gray crushed shell pad.

"Over there, by Wade's personal shuttle." Eleanor pointed to a small knot of people standing at the bottom of the farthest shuttle's ramp.

Harriet recognized Tarbell and Alex and Payson's personal pilot; a short, dark man who looked out of place without his uniform. The shuttle pilots and crew lived in employee housing on the island and helped out where needed when not on standby to fly, but Harriet rarely saw them unless she made a trip to the mainland.

She parked the Hog near the shuttle's nose, attached Belle's leash to her collar, and approached the group.

"Doctor. Thank you for responding so fast. In here." Alex led Eleanor up the ramp and into the shuttle before Harriet could ask him why they needed a doctor.

Except for the group next to Payson's shuttle, the pad and buildings appeared to be deserted. Inactivated droids stood in a double line inside the open-walled waiting area. They were shut down each Saturday after the last guest arrived and reactivated for the guests' departure and new arrivals a week later. In between times they stood as silent sentinels for the deserted pad.

Unlike the pink shell road which reflected the sun's rays, the blue-gray shell pad absorbed the sun's heat, making it a good ten degrees warmer than the surrounding jungle. The high-pitched buzz of the heat-loving insects high in the trees made Harriet feel even hotter. She took Belle to the shaded bar and waiting area and secured her leash to a table leg.

"Stay," she commanded. She had no idea if Belle understood the command, but she was worried the pad might be too hot for the dog's feet. Fortunately, Belle seemed content to lie in the shade and Harriet hurried back to Payson's shuttle.

"What's going on?" she demanded. "Neither Alex nor Eleanor would tell me anything."

"Mr. Douglas asked me to ready the shuttle for a trip to the mainland later this afternoon," Rod answered. "Apparently one of the rescued missing women wants to return to the mainland immediately. When I arrived, I found the shuttle unlocked."

"That's bad." Harriet frowned. "I thought it was impossible to get inside one once they're locked." The shuttles had sophisticated locking systems and were kept secured when not in use to prevent any teens or drunken guests from trying to fly one of the resort's ultra modern birds.

"Is someone in there now?"

"Our kidnapper hid the women inside the shuttle."

"What? Oh, crap." No wonder Tarbell looked so disgusted. They had searched the waiting area and mechanic's building, but no one had bothered to search the shuttles for the missing women because they couldn't be accessed. Or so they had thought.

"How did the kidnapper get in?"

"He had to have used a decoder. Homemade, as there's nothing on the market that could breach the Wade Industry security system on these shuttles."

"If he had a decoder that could explain how he entered Azzi and Angela's rooms without being heard."

"Exactly."

"Is Eleanor here because Angela is still inside the shuttle?" The last woman kidnapped and the only one not returned, Harriet wondered what kind of shape the escort worker was in.

"The bedroom was locked. When I opened it I found a young woman lying on the boss's bed, asleep," Rod said. "I couldn't wake her. That's when I called Alex."

He looked and sounded distraught. "I hope she's going to be all right."

They all stared at the door at the top of the ramp stairs as if willing Angela to appear.

"I haven't seen her yet, but Alex said he thinks she's under the influence of Blitz." Tarbell pinched the bridge of his nose. "This is a real bring down. We still have no idea who the kidnapper is and the guests will be leaving in two days. He might just get away with it."

"At least all the victims have been found alive," Harriet pointed out. "That's better than having another murder on our hands." If the situation hadn't been so serious she would have grinned at the disgusted look Tarbell shot her.

"I'd rather everyone was all right *and* we caught the perp, thank you very much."

Another ten minutes passed before Eleanor appeared at the head of the ramp with Alex behind her carrying an awake Angela Daly.

Harriet squelched the sudden spurt of jealousy when the woman wrapped her arms around Alex's neck and chided herself for feeling so petty. She should be ecstatic that Fitness Girl had been found alive and obviously well. Of course Alex was carrying her–the poor woman was probably too weak to walk.

Angela laid her head against Alex's chest and the jealousy burned a little hotter.

"She seems more alert than the other two," Harriet remarked drily.

"The kidnapper had her less time than Patricia or Azzi, so less Blitz in her system." Tarbell moved forward to meet the doctor and Alex at the bottom of the ramp.

"Are you feeling well enough to return to the hotel?" he asked Angela.

"I think so," she replied in a weak voice.

"She's in better shape than the other two," Eleanor said, "and she wants to get back to her rooms to let her friend know she's okay, so I'd say yes. Let's take her to the hotel. I'll finish checking her over there."

Alex placed Angela in the second Hog's rear seat. Eleanor joined her and Tarbell slipped behind the wheel.

"I'll ride with Harriet," Alex said, disengaging Angela's arms from his neck. "We'll meet you at the hotel shortly."

"Can I clean the shuttle now?" Rod asked him, once the others had gone. "The women, they, uh, apparently weren't able to use the bathroom while they were being held and it's a bit ripe inside the main cabin."

"I want to take a quick look first, see if our kidnapper left anything behind that might help us identify him."

"Fair enough. I'll be in the maintenance building. Just give me a shout when you've finished." Rod walked away a few steps, then turned back. "By the way, Harry, I'm happy to see you look a sight better than you did last time I saw you." He grinned and headed off.

Since Rod had flown her to the resort from Apple Valley right after she'd spent the night watching Margaret Blackstone's cabin burn, Harriet knew he spoke the truth. She'd been bleary-eyed, covered in soot, and reeked of smoke that day; unable to clean up until she returned to the island.

"Thanks for getting Eleanor." Alex placed a light kiss on her lips and Harriet immediately felt better and at the same time ashamed that she'd been jealous of the rescued woman.

"You're welcome. Can I come inside with you while you search?"

"As long as you don't touch anything. Although you may not want to stay once you get inside. Rod wasn't exaggerating when he said it was ripe in there."

"Poor women." She followed Alex up the ramp and stopped in the open doorway. The smell hit her before she even stepped inside the cabin: a pungent blend of acrid urine, feces, and sour sweat.

"Ugh."

"Why don't you wait in the shade with Belle? I won't be long; I just want to take a quick look, see if our kidnapper might have left something behind other than Angela. I'll do a more thorough search with Fox after we take her statement."

"I'm okay."

She wanted to see where the women had been kept. She couldn't explain why she felt the need to understand what it was like for Patricia and Azzi and Angela, but she did. They'd been trussed up and held in the dark. Helpless. It was the helpless part that frightened her the most. How did they feel when they realized there was nothing they could do to help themselves?

Two pair of cut black zip ties lay in the aisle; one set forward and one near the door to Payson's bedroom. Empty tubes of water and discarded pressure syringes littered the floor. Harriet rubbed her breastbone, trying to ease the sudden pressure in her chest.

"It looks like the kidnapper secured Azzi and Patricia in the main cabin," she said. "Why not put them all in the bedroom? Or why put Angela in the bedroom and not in the cabin?"

"It looks as if our guy wanted to keep the women separate. Maybe to keep them from realizing they weren't alone." He walked to the rear of the shuttle and entered the bedroom.

"I think they were too drugged to realize anything," Harriet murmured, counting the syringes on the cabin floor. They would have been incapable of the simplest action, drugged to the gills as they must have been.

A wave of nausea washed over her. She turned and leaned against the edge of the doorway so she could catch the fresh breeze. The nausea passed after a few minutes, but she remained in the doorway.

"You know what I don't get?" she called. "Why even take Angela? She's a sex worker, not a millionaire. You would assume the kidnapper researched his targets once he got here. He would know Angela wasn't worth the effort."

Alex came out of the bedroom. "That's a very good point. I'm done here for now. Let's head to the hotel. I want to speak with Angela."

"What about the shuttle?"

"Rod will be here. I'll activate a few droids and set them to guard it in case the kidnapper returns."

They had just passed the fork in the road when Alex's link buzzed.

"Fox. What is it?"

When he put the link away without saying anything else, Harriet gave him a curious look.

"Well? What did Tarbell want?"

"Angela's roommate is dead."

CHAPTER TWENTY

"Angela's roommate is dead."

The words reverberated inside Harriet's head. She closed her eyes briefly. She'd jumped the gun when she had told Tarbell that, while kidnapping was bad enough, at least they didn't have a murder on their hands.

"Why would anyone want Rodney Lynch dead?" Harriet stared at Alex. "I don't get it. Rodney Lynch is dead? What happened?"

"Let's just get to the hotel. This is turning into the craziest week we've had here yet." Crossing his arms over his chest, Alex stared out the Hog's side window.

Harriet didn't ask any more questions. She concentrated on driving them to the hotel, knowing that Alex's brain was churning over the few facts they had managed to glean about the kidnapper. How Fitness Guy fit in was a mystery.

Kidnapped, rescued, and now her friend and sometime co-worker was dead—Angela had to be reeling from the shock of recent events.

She parked the Hog in front of the hotel, lowered all the windows part way for Belle, and hurried after Alex, who was already up the stairs and halfway down the hall leading to the Fitness Couple's suite by the time she caught him.

Tarbell answered Alex's sharp rap so fast Harriet knew he must have been waiting at the door for them. Alex strode into the room with Harriet on his heels and Tarbell shut the door behind them.

"In there." Tarbell nodded toward Rodney's bedroom.

Alex placed a hand on Harriet's arm. "You might want to wait out here."

She didn't really want to wait alone in the suite's sitting room. Then again, she didn't really want to see another body either, especially since she didn't know how Rodney Lynch had died. She pictured blood sprayed on the walls and gory body parts strewn around the bedroom and shuddered. No, she most definitely didn't want to see that.

Gingerly, she sniffed the air. Thankfully there was no coppery smell of blood. She chided herself for letting her imagination run away with her but made no move to follow Alex and Tarbell.

Female voices came from Angela's room on the opposite side of the sitting, drawing Harriet closer. Standing outside the partially closed door, she debated whether to intrude on Eleanor's examination of the rescued woman.

"I can't believe he's dead. Rodney is my best friend in the whole world. We often worked together, you know. There was no one I'd rather get naked with."

"Ew." Harriet clapped her hand over her mouth to muffle her reaction. A picture of Fitness Couple with their perfect, plastic doll bodies working out a sex routine popped into her brain—and weirded her out.

"I'm very sorry for your loss but we need to focus on you now." Eleanor sounded sympathetic but brisk. "I'd like to take a blood sample to test for Blitz if you don't mind. We'll use it to help build a case against the kidnapper when he's caught."

"No. You're not taking my blood."

Harriet moved a few steps closer to the door.

"I assure you, it won't hurt a bit."

"No." Angela's voice rose in a panic. "I can't stand the sight of blood and you can't force me to give it to you. Not going to happen. My best friend has been murdered. You should be in there helping Alex find out what happened, not trying to jab me with needles so you can drain my body."

"As you wish. I can't force you to give me a sample. Lie back on the pillows, please, Miss Daly. I won't take your blood if you don't want me to, I promise." Despite the soft tone, Harriet heard Eleanor's frustration.

Thinking the doctor might need some reinforcement, Harriet rapped lightly on the door and stuck her head around the edge. Angela sat propped up against a pile of pillows, her blonde hair done in a thick braid that hung nearly to her waist. She had changed into a pink tank top that emphasized her well-toned arms, firm breasts, and smooth tan.

Unlike the other two kidnap victims, who looked like they'd been through a rough ordeal, Angela merely looked tired, with faint purple shadows underscoring her large, pale green eyes.

Eleanor stood at Angela's bedside, her lips pressed together into a firm line. She clearly was not happy with her uncooperative patient. Harriet pasted on a bright smile and stepped into the room.

"Hi, Angela. Do you remember me? I'm Harriet Monroe, director of public relations for the resort. How are you feeling? Is there anything I can do or get for you?"

Angela snorted. "Public relations? You have your work cut out for you. As soon as I hit the mainland I'm going straight to the news services to tell them how dangerous this place is." She looked more closely at Harriet and narrowed her eyes.

"Wait a minute. You're the woman who helped that cop search

our room. As if Rodney would ever kidnap anybody. Obviously you were wrong. Bet you feel bad about that now that Rod's been murdered." A well-timed tear rolled down her cheek.

"I'm sorry for your loss, and I apologize for any inconvenience we may have caused you at the time, Miss Daly. Mr. Fox and I had to search every room in the hotel, not just yours, so please don't take it personally."

"Whatever. Unless you can bring Rod back, there's nothing you can do for me. I'd like to be alone now if you don't mind."

Harriet looked at Eleanor, who shrugged.

"We'll be right outside in the sitting room," Eleanor told her. "If you need anything, don't hesitate to call out." She joined Harriet and partially closed the door to Angela's room behind them. Moving away from the door, she motioned to Harriet to join her.

"What do you think?" Harriet asked, keeping her voice low so Angela wouldn't overhear. "How is she, Doctor?"

"She's in remarkably good shape compared to Miss Williams and Miss DeBerry. But then, she was in superior physical condition to start with and wasn't held for as long, so I'd expected her to be in better shape."

"Yeah, she looked pretty healthy to me." Harriet reached for the lanai door but Eleanor stopped her.

"We have a suspicious death. Don't touch anything."

Harriet flushed. She knew better than to touch anything and shouldn't have needed Eleanor to remind her.

"Eleanor! Can you come in here?" The summons came from Rodney's room, not Angela's. Harriet followed Eleanor as far as the bedroom door, where she stopped to take in the scene before her.

Rodney lay on his back on his bed, dressed in running shorts and a white tee that lay snugly against his well-developed chest. His feet were bare. Harriet looked over her shoulder to the suite door; a pair of trainers sat neatly next to the door. She returned her attention to the body on the bed.

If not for the dry, dull look in his half-closed eyes, Rodney looked as if he could be taking a nap. Taking in his perfect body and handsome face, she had to admit that he must have been a very popular licensed companion, with plenty of repeat clients.

Alex stood beside him, frowning down at a leopard print link in his gloved hand, one she recognized as the same link Rodney had used to call Angela when she went missing.

A pair of khakis, a bright white polo shirt, and navy-colored briefs lay neatly folded on the chair next to the bathroom door. A leather belt lay rolled on top of the clothing and a pair of leather sandals sat precisely side by side beneath the chair. The rest of the room was pristine, just as it had looked when she and Tarbell had first searched the hotel for the kidnapped guests.

"Eleanor, take a look at the vic and tell me what you see." Alex moved away from the bed and the doctor took his place.

"I'd say he's been dead maybe six hours, give or take an hour. Best guess, he died from a drug overdose," she said after a few minutes.

Harriet made a startled sound. The others looked at her.

"Sorry. It's just—I'm surprised. Rodney treated his body like a temple. I would have sworn that he never touched drugs."

"Apparently he touched them plenty since he's been at the resort." Alex wiggled the link in his hand. "This is Rodney's link. The last thing on it is a suicide note. He apologizes for all the trouble he's caused and claims that he knows he did wrong and wants to set things right but can't face prison."

He dropped the link into his pocket. "Looks like we have our kidnapper. I'm going to speak to Angela, see if she had any idea her roommate was kidnapping young women and holding them for ransom."

"Does he mention returning the money?" Harriet asked, thinking of Azzi and Patricia, who had lost everything.

Alex frowned. "No. I'll have to dig deeper into the link to see if there are any bank transfers on there."

He stopped at the door. "Eleanor, will you come with me in case Angela becomes upset?"

"Of course."

Curious to hear Angela's reaction to the news her friend was the kidnapper, Harriet followed behind. Alex stood on one side of Angela's bed with Eleanor opposite.

"I have bad news," Alex began. "It seems that Rodney Lynch was our kidnapper."

"No. I don't believe it." Angela shook her head. "He would never do something like that. He would never kidnap *me*."

Alex pulled Rodney's link from his pocket and showed the message to Angela.

"Oh, no." Several large tears spilled from her eyes. "I can't believe it." She sniffed and dabbed at her eyes with a dainty white handkerchief embroidered with a pink A.

Of course she had a handkerchief. The woman was the epitome of feminine. She made Harriet feel about as graceful and feminine as a dancing bear.

Harriet chided herself that Angela worked hard at the illusion that she was the perfect woman. It was a necessary part of her job, after all, and probably a persona she kept up twenty-four/seven. She'd just lost her good friend. Harriet should be feeling sympathetic toward the woman, not criticizing her.

She huffed out a quiet sigh. Feeling inferior to smaller, more feminine women was a failing in her own character that she needed to address. There were always going to be smaller, more feminine women; it was time she accepted that and stopped resenting them. They couldn't help their physical stature any more than she could.

Alex took Angela's hand and sat on the edge of the bed. "I'm truly sorry. I suspect Rodney needed to get you out of the way for a while. Kidnapping you also threw us off his trail."

When Angela's lower lip began to quiver, Harriet decided she didn't want to watch any more. Crossing the sitting room, she stood in Rodney's doorway and stared into his room, chewing at the inside of her cheek. Something bugged her about the room.

"Have you found anything?" she asked Tarbell, who stood at the foot of the bed after searching the bathroom.

"Only these." He held up a small evidence bag containing two pressure syringes. "They were in the bathroom trash. Other than these, doodely-squat. The bathroom is pristine, his body and hair products lined up neatly and perfectly clean. The sink is dry, towels neatly folded and stacked. It looks just like it did when we searched the place for Angela."

Had Rodney been obsessive compulsive? It certainly looked that way. Harriet scanned the room. Nothing was out of place. Her gaze returned to the pile of neatly folded clothing beside the bathroom door. She realized what was bothering her and pointed to the clothes.

"Doesn't it seem odd that a man who was planning to commit suicide would lay out the clothes he intended to dress in after his run and shower? Why bother if he knew he was going to kill himself? Or, why not shower and change before he offed himself? Rodney was methodical. Regimented. If he laid out his clothes, then he intended to wear them."

Tarbell shrugged. "I've seen stranger things; but yeah, you could be right. It's worth considering." Turning a slow circle, he surveyed the room. "If he didn't commit suicide, then he was murdered. Why?"

"To make him a scapegoat," Harriet answered promptly. "Kill Rodney, leave the suicide note on his link, and make us believe he was the kidnapper so we'd stop looking. I honestly don't believe

Rodney would voluntarily put drugs into his body. He worked too hard to keep it looking good to abuse himself like that. I'd bet my hippo collection that Rodney did not commit suicide."

Tarbell looked amused. "You feel that strongly, huh? It's a plausible theory, but remember, people will do unexpected and out of character things when they're desperate. Rodney had a supply of Blitz. It's an easy way out. Take an overdose of the drug and essentially go to sleep. No pain. No messing up his pretty face and body."

Just like what Margaret Blackstone had done to the cult members–fed them an overdose of a slow-acting poison.Harriet suppressed a shudder and forced herself to focus. She wasn't ready to give up the argument that Rodney wouldn't put drugs in his body.

"Alex said the last thing on Rodney's link was a note apologizing for all the trouble he's caused."

"Yeah. You heard him. Rodney said he knew he did wrong and wants to set things right. Your point?"

"What if it wasn't a suicide note, but had to do with something else? Those words could apply to anything–something with a client, for example. Being a high class escort can't be easy; I'm sure he had the occasional dissatisfied customer. Maybe he was trying to mend fences."

Tarbell still looked unconvinced. Harriet pressed further.

"If he was the kidnapper, then why did he kidnap Angela?"

"To throw us off. To make us regard him with sympathy instead of suspicion."

Alex appeared next to Harriet before she could disagree with Tarbell's argument.

"Fox. Captain Rod found something while cleaning the shuttle's bedroom. I'm going to run up there on my bike. I want you to stay here with Angela until I get back."

"Do you want me to stick around?" Harriet asked. "I need to get Belle from the Hog if I'm going to be much longer."

"You can take Eleanor back to the spa when she's ready. I won't be long. If you head to the office let me know. Otherwise I'll worry." He kissed her and was gone.

Despite her refusal to marry him, Alex acted as if nothing had changed between them. He either had supreme confidence that she would change her mind and ask him to marry her, or . . . There was no or. Alex believed in their future together. She found his confidence comforting.

"I wonder what Rod found," Tarbell mused, bringing her back to the bedroom and the body on the bed. "It'd have to be damned interesting for Alex to run off like that when he has a fresh witness to interview."

"Whatever it is, let's hope it answers some questions." Harriet crossed the sitting room to Angela's bedroom and poked her head in.

Angela lay with her eyes closed, her hands folded on her stomach. Her skin looked dewy and smooth—obviously well cared for, just like her body. Harriet wondered how often she had it treated. Weekly? Monthly? The treatments were a business expense and necessary if Angela wanted to attract the highest level of clientele.

Rubbing the edge of her hand over her own cheek, Harriet noticed that it felt dry and slightly rough. She'd been lax lately on body care. She needed to start taking better care of her skin before the tropical sun did too much damage. Maybe regular trips to the spa . . .

Disgusted by the direction of her thoughts, she dropped her hand. She'd never been obsessed with her looks and wasn't about to start now. She looked at Angela's dewy skin again. Perhaps she could strike a happy medium. After all, she didn't want to end up with the tough, mottled lizard skin she'd seen on some of the resort's older sun-worshipping guests.

Eleanor had abandoned her post beside Angela's bed and stood at the bedroom's lanai doors, watching the guests milling in front of the hotel. She turned when Harriet cleared her throat.

"Do you need a ride back to the spa?" Harriet asked in a loud whisper.

The doctor gave a curt nod, gathered her bag, and joined Harriet and Tarbell in the sitting room, closing Angela's door behind her. Tarbell reopened it partway.

"I need to keep an eye on her," he explained. "What did she say when Alex told her that her friend Rodney was the kidnapper?"

"She denied it, until Alex showed her the message on Rodney's link. Then she cried. I gave her a mild sedative so she'll sleep for a while. Give me a call if she seems agitated when she wakes." She gave Tarbell a curt nod and left the suite with Harriet on her heels.

When they approached the Hog, Belle barked and greeted Harriet like a long lost loved one. She whined and wiggled her whole body, jumped out of the Hog, then back in again, making little yips the whole time.

"I love that Belle is so happy to see me, but I feel so bad whenever I leave her," Harriet complained. "I'm afraid she has abandonment issues."

Eleanor laughed and told her to get used to it. "She'll be that happy to see you whether you've been out of her sight for several days or five minutes. It's a dog's way."

After dropping Eleanor off at the spa, Harriet sat in the Hog for several minutes debating where to go next. The work day was nearly over and she had zero interest in starting up a project in her office. She decided to head back to Angela and Rodney's suite to talk to Tarbell and started the Hog, but her link buzzed before she could put it in gear.

"Harry? It's Fox. Could you come back to the hotel after you drop off Eleanor? I'd like a female here when Angela wakes up."

Harriet smirked. "Don't tell me you're afraid of Fitness Girl. She does know Krav Maga, but I think you can take her–especially in her weakened state."

"Ha-ha. I need a witness in case she claims I tried to take advantage of her."

That wiped the smirk off Harriet's face. "Why would she do that?"

Tarbell hedged. "I'm just being cautious. You coming?"

Narrowing her eyes, Harriet tried to understand why Tarbell needed her there. The truth struck.

"You think that something feels off about Rodney's suicide, too, don't you?"

"Yeah. I've been going through his link and there's nothing here that I'd expect to find if he was the kidnapper. No background research on the victims. No offshore bank account. Nothing in his room or luggage. The guy seemed to be one hundred percent completely focused on his job as a licensed companion."

"I just dropped Eleanor off. I'll be there in under ten."

"Great. Thanks."

Harriet reached the main road and goosed the Hog's throttle.

They were both thinking along the same groove. If Rodney Lynch had been the kidnapper he must have had help. Who better than his friend Angela?

CHAPTER TWENTY-ONE

When she reached the hotel, Belle leaped from the Hog before Harriet could shut her in.

"All right. I don't particularly want to leave you behind anyway." She attached Belle's leash and headed inside with the dog trotting happily beside her.

The lobby teemed with guests. They filled the seating areas nestled among the large flower arrangements that Solly and his crew changed out every few days, chatting with friends and family or reading. Families with children dressed in bright beach wear called to one another to grab towels, get drinks and snacks, where's your brother?

It was noisy, chaotic, and colorful. Everyone looked relaxed and happy, unaware of the drama of the past few days. For a brief moment, Harriet wished she could join them in their ignorance, then she headed to the second floor to meet Tarbell in Angela and Rodney's suite.

Tarbell answered her knock immediately, closing the door behind them with a soft click.

"Is Angela still sleeping?"

"She was right before I called you. I haven't checked on her since."

Harriet glanced toward Rodney's bedroom door.

"His body's been moved to Eleanor's new refrigeration unit."

Harriet suppressed a shudder. Bodies needed to be protected from the heat until they could be transported to the mainland's medical examiner's office. After the last murder, the resort doctor had requested a special refrigerator—one she hoped never to have to use. They couldn't put dead bodies in the kitchens' refrigerators or freezers—who would want to eat food that had sat alongside a decomposing body—no matter how lovingly prepared? The thought was abhorrent.

"Alex called a few minutes ago. Captain Rod found the decoder our kidnapper used hidden in the bathroom towels. He says it looks like a commercial model."

"Not homemade?"

"Definitely not homemade. The question is, where did Rodney get it?"

Tarbell opened the lanai doors. A light breeze filled the curtains and stirred the loose hairs around Harriet's face. She stared out at a pale gray fog bank on the horizon and pondered the question. How would an LC learn about security systems?

"One of his clients," she said aloud, turning her head to look at Tarbell, who had sprawled in one of the deep, cushioned chairs. "Pillow talk. Isn't that what they call it when spies seduce their target to get classified information from them?"

"I've never met a spy, but I agree that a client is the most likely source. We'll see what Angela has to say when Alex gets here and we show her the device."

Something niggled at Harriet's brain, something about the decoder being found in the unlocked plane, but the thought eluded her and she let it go. Experience had taught her that if the thought was important it would come back. She took the chair near Tarbell and they waited for Alex in a companionable silence.

Harriet didn't realize she'd nodded off until Belle's soft "Woof!" woke her. Tarbell was already at the door. Payson entered with Alex on his heels and settled on a chair near Harriet with a quiet hello. Tarbell checked on Angela and closed the door to her room before joining them.

The atmosphere in the room had turned somber. The ramifications of finding the decoder went far beyond the kidnappings. If a company was producing instruments that could neutralize top of the line security systems, then no one would be safe.

Payson pulled a black box smaller than a deck of cards from his pocket and handed it to Tarbell.

"Have you seen anything like this before?" Tarbell asked, turning the decoder over in his hands.

"I have, actually. It's a prototype Wade's lab recently created at the request of the government."

Harriet frowned. "Wow. What's it doing on the resort?"

Payson's eyes were icy with anger. "Obviously it was stolen from the lab. Which means that someone who worked on the prototype took it and sold it. Why it hasn't been reported yet is something I'll be pursuing as soon as we finish here."

That was bad. Harriet knew Payson wouldn't rest until he'd found and punished the technician who'd dared to steal from him. He paid extraordinarily well and worked hard to develop employee loyalty. Once found, the culprit would never work in research and development again–and would certainly serve time in prison.

She held out her hand and Tarbell dropped the decoder into her palm. It had more heft than she'd expected, while being small and slim enough to easily fit in a pocket. A narrow screen filled part the top, with rows of ridges beneath. She pushed one experimentally and the screen lit up.

Running her fingers over the smooth bottom surface, she felt something raised on the underside. She traced the tiny, stylized WI set in one corner. She handed the decoder back to Payson.

"Harry and I have a theory," Tarbell said, after everyone had checked out the decoder. "One, we don't think Rodney was working alone." He jerked his head toward Angela's door.

"Two, we think one of them acquired the decoder from a client—either stole it or sweet talked them into lending it to them."

Alex smiled grimly. "I think it's time we woke Angela up and asked a few pointed questions."

It took Angela ten minutes to dress and join them. She'd put on form-fitted pink capris with a matching sleeveless tee that stopped well shy of her navel, and combed out her thick, blonde hair. The pink highlighted her smooth tan while making her look feminine and vulnerable.

"Sit here, Angela." Alex led her to one of the cushioned chairs. Tarbell had moved to a spot standing in front of the lanai doors, while Payson and Harriet sat side by side on the couch.

Alex pulled a hardback chair from the table and set it in front of Angela. He sat, set his forearms on his thighs, and laced his fingers together. For a long moment, he said nothing while he observed her.

Harriet marveled at Angela's composure. If she'd been in Angela's position, she would have been fidgeting under Alex's silent treatment. Not Angela. The licensed companion merely looked bored.

"Angela, how long had you and Rodney known each?"

"Seven, maybe eight years. I've already told you this."

Alex ignored her comment. "During those seven or eight years, did Rodney ever commit a crime? To the best of your knowledge."

"No. I would have said that Rodney was as straight as they

come." Her pale green eyes welled with tears. Harriet wondered if crying was something she had learned to do at will.

"That's why I was so shocked to learn that he was the kidnapper. Doubly shocked that he had kidnapped *me*."

Alex leaned back in the chair and stretched out one leg. "See, that's what I'm having trouble with."

"I don't understand." Harriet wondered if she was imagining the note of wariness that had crept into Angela's voice.

"I'm asking myself why Rodney would kidnap you."

"To keep me quiet, obviously."

"So you knew what he was doing."

"No. I–"

"Otherwise, why would he need to keep you quiet if you didn't suspect anything?"

"I don't know what Rod was thinking. He couldn't risk me finding out. And maybe he wanted to throw off any suspicions you might have had." Angela pulled her silky curtain of blonde hair to the side and let it drape over one breast as she nodded.

"Knowing Rod, I'm sure that's why he kidnapped me."

Alex nodded. "Plausible." He reached out a hand toward Payson. Payson dropped the decoder into it.

Harriet saw a quick flash of panic in Angela's eyes, and realized what had been bugging her. Why would the kidnapper leave the decoder in the shuttle? It was a valuable piece of equipment, far too valuable to leave behind. That meant the kidnapper had been forced to hide it when she was caught in the shuttle.

Alex's next words told her that he had worked out the same logic.

"We have reason to believe that Rodney wasn't working alone, Angela." He toyed with the decoder, turning it over and over in his land.

Angela sat perfectly still, like a rabbit trying to hide from a fox, hoping it wouldn't be noticed if it didn't move.

"Captain Rod found this interesting piece of equipment stuffed into the towels in the shuttle's master bath. Have you ever seen it before?"

Angela crossed her arms over her chest. "No. Why would I? I was a prisoner, remember?"

Alex continued as if she hadn't spoken. "Well, here's the thing; this little decoder is a prototype from one of Wade Industries' labs–a prototype that was stolen."

Beneath her tan, Angela blanched when she heard Wade's name. Alex nodded.

"So you can see why we're all very curious as to how this stolen piece of technology ended up on the island. Would you care to hazard a guess?"

"How should I know?" She lifted one smooth shoulder and tried to look disinterested, but Harriet could see the rapid beat of her pulse in her neck. Angela never took her eyes off Alex–a rat mesmerized by a cobra it knows will strike any moment.

"Here's the thing, Angela. I know the kidnapper couldn't have left this behind, because then he couldn't lock and unlock the shuttle. Which means . . ."

Angela's lips parted slightly as she waited for Alex to finish the sentence.

He turned his head to look at Tarbell, who, Harriet now noticed, had been working a slim black link that looked exactly like Angela's link.

"Fox?"

"It's all here, boss. Bank transfers from Patricia's and Azzi's accounts into an account in the Cayman Islands."

Alex turned back to Angela. She pressed her lips together.

"I'd like to know how you came to possess the decoder," Payson told her.

Harriet watched the calculation behind those pale green eyes.

"I want a deal. No jail time."

Didn't the woman realize no one in the room had the power to offer her a deal? She wouldn't even be charged until she was handed over to the authorities on the mainland.

"Azzi and Patricia are decent people," Tarbell said smoothly. "If you agree to return all of their money they'll probably drop any kidnapping charges."

Angela looked pained, then resigned. She rattled off a string of numbers. "That's the number and passcode for the Cayman account. You can reverse the transfers."

"The decoder." Harriet heard the steel in Payson's voice. Apparently Angela did as well.

"The night before we left the mainland I had a booking with a client who does a lot of classified software design. He has a crush on me and always tries to impress me with his projects. He showed me this instrument he claimed he had designed that he said could get through any security lock." She pointed to the decoder.

"That was in his briefcase. I played dumb and asked him to show me how it worked."

"He gave it to you?" Payson sounded incredulous. Harriet had to agree. The decoder was like a magic key that could open any door, any vault.

"No. I drugged him, tied him up, and took the decoder. My first idea was to rob the resort hotel safes, but then I'd have to move anything I stole off the island to fence and I couldn't see any easy way to do that, so I canned that plan." Confident she would get off without doing prison time, Angela had decided to talk. She continued her story unprompted.

"Then I hit on kidnapping and demanding a ransom. I figure your guests can afford it. I bought a bunch of pressure syringes loaded with Blitz to keep them quiet, and once we arrived on the island I talked Rodney into helping me kidnap those two women.

He didn't like it, but I've always been able to get him to do what I want."

"I'll need a name and description of the man with the decoder," Alex told her.

"Of course. Anything to help." She sounded cheerful. Her body language had relaxed; her arms no longer crossed over her breasts.

"When did you decide to kill Rodney?"

"What? I didn't–"

Alex talked right over her. "I think you found the note he wrote on his link and realized he was going to confess your sins. It wasn't a suicide note, was it? What happened?"

"He was my friend. I would never–"

"You might as well fess up, Angela," Tarbell said. "We found your prints on the syringes you used to overdose your roommate."

Harriet gave him a sharp look. She could have sworn the syringes he had found in Rodney's bathroom trash had been wiped clean.

"I should have known he didn't have the balls to follow my plan through to the end." The contempt in Angela's voice jarred. She crossed her legs and swung her foot.

"He wanted to give the money all back. Said he felt sorry for the women because they'd lost their families and were alone in the world. Well, boo-hoo. They had more than enough money to make up for no mommy or daddy–and no siblings they had to share it with."

"You couldn't bear to give the money back. So you gave your friend an overdose of Blitz."

Angela shrugged. "He shoulda gone along with the plan."

Harriet had heard enough. Angela's callousness and lack of feeling and respect for someone who was supposed to be her closest friend had shaken and depressed her. She told Alex she was headed home and excused herself.

As she maneuvered through the guests she wondered how a person could become so callous. What was Angela's back story? She supposed it would all come out at Angela's trial, but she wouldn't follow it. Life had enough depressing moments in it without seeking out the darkness that resided in some people.

CHAPTER TWENTY-TWO

Harriet's link buzzed before she'd made it halfway home. She had rolled down the windows and both her and Belle were enjoying the warm breeze flowing through the Hog. Sunlight reflected off the dark gray bodies of a pod of dolphins playing in the water. One flipped a fish into the air and caught it. The scene made her smile.

There was more than enough beauty in the world to offset the ugliness if she took the time to look and appreciate it. Her link vibrated in her pocket.

"Harry? It's William. We need to talk. Can you meet me at your cottage?"

"What's this about?"

"I'd rather talk in person." He sounded tense.

"I'm almost home. I'll see you in a few."

Why did William want—no, *need*—to talk to her. Had he seen her drive away when he and O'Claire had been arguing?

Harriet worried over William's call the remainder of the drive to the cottages. He must have seen her—it was the only explanation. He'd sounded so tense.

Or had Solly tagged him and told him about her visit and

their argument? A hard knot formed in her stomach. She hated confrontations.

She expected to see William waiting for her outside Venus Cottage, but the parking pad was empty. Pulling next door, she parked the Hog behind Mermaid, let Belle out, and walked to the front of the cottages. There was no sign of William. He had said he'd meet her at the cottage. So where was he?

When William had called, he'd made her think they needed to speak right away. Had she misunderstood? She pulled out her link and tagged him, but it went straight to message.

Harriet knocked on Venus's back door. "William! I'm here. Where are you?" She waited, growing more impatient by the minute. What kind of game was William playing?

Harriet knocked again, walked around the cottage, then gave up. "I'm not waiting around any longer. Let's go for a run, Belle."

Now that the kidnappers had been identified and caught, there was no reason not to return to her normal activities. Running helped her relax, and after the earlier scene with Angela she felt wired. She needed to pound the sand and draw the fresh salt air into her lungs.

Alex and Tarbell and Payson would be tied up for a while, wringing as much information from Angela as possible. She decided not to call Alex. She'd be back and showered before he even knew she'd gone.

Twenty minutes later, she reset Mermaid's alarm and stepped off her lanai with Belle at her side. A group of sleek, black seal heads popped to the surface in the waves not far off shore. There was no sign of the dolphins she's seen earlier. Beyond the seals floated a large yacht with a gleaming white hull. She idly wondered what it would be like to travel the world in a ship that size, making the sea your home and only touching land when you needed supplies.

She suspected the life of a nomad would lose its appeal after a while. People needed to be rooted someplace, to have a home to return to. Or a person to return to.

In the past that had always meant Solly for her. They'd lived in dozens of apartments together–moving whenever a landlord raised the rent or their circumstances improved enough to afford better digs. But as long as Solly was there, no matter how shabby or unfamiliar the surroundings, the place felt like home. She hoped she'd be able to build that same sense of home with Alex.

Movement on the right caught her eye and she turned to see Martin O'Claire coming toward her from the beach.

"Harry! I was hoping to run into you. I recently heard about your orphan program and wonder if there's any way I can contribute. It sounds like a worthy cause."

Politeness and the desperate desire to get moving in the fresh sea air warred in Harriet's chest.

"I was going for a run, Mr. O'Claire. Could we meet up to talk later?" she asked.

"I'll come with you," Martin replied. "I haven't put in my miles yet today." He must have noticed something on her face because he was quick to add, "If I can't keep up, I promise I'll turn around and catch you later. Okay?"

Embarrassed that he'd read her so easily, Harriet reluctantly agreed. They headed down to the wet, harder sand and began a slow jog toward the mangrove swamp at the southern tip of the island. The preacher shortened his longer stride to match Harriet's and they ran side by side in silence for several minutes. When she felt warmed up, Harriet kicked up the pace, hoping the preacher would turn back.

Unfortunately, he had no difficulty keeping up with her.

"What would you like to know about my orphans?"

"I'm curious about how the program started. How did you happen to think of bringing them here? For most people, orphans are out of sight, out of mind."

"That's easy. I was an orphan. My parents both died when I was eight, only unlike the orphans we bring here, I had a relative who was willing to take me in. I wanted to do something to give the ones who have no family hope, to show that someone was aware of their plight and was willing to do something about it."

"That sounds like a big undertaking."

"I've had a lot of support. Obviously I can't find adoptive parents for them all, but once they come here we try to pair them up with a sponsor. The sponsors commit to helping the children get a solid education and make sure their material needs are met until they're able to care for themselves. The best sponsors go beyond that and become mentors and friends, which is my ultimate goal. A child only needs one person in their life who believes in them to withstand all the crap life can throw at them."

"You sound as if you speak from experience."

The familiar sweet-rotten, brackish scent of the swamp carried on the breeze as they neared the forest of mangroves that covered the southern tip of the island. They ran in silence until they reached the end of the open beach.

"Fascinating places, mangrove swamps," Martin said, slowing to a walk. "It's an impenetrable ecosystem with a huge diversity of wildlife and sea creatures. I found some blue soldier crabs here yesterday. They're quite beautiful. Let me show you."

He plunged into the water and waded toward the thick, tangled roots of a mangrove tree.

Harriet hesitated. She didn't really care about the crabs, but she also didn't want to be rude. On the other hand, what did she know about Martin O'Claire? She searched the beach and saw a couple walking toward her, still a fair distance away–certainly too far to hear a shout for help. The yacht hadn't moved and she couldn't see anyone on its decks watching the shore.

"Don't be so paranoid," she said under her breath. The man

was just being friendly. Alex had checked O'Claire out and learned nothing alarming.

"Harry!" Martin beckoned her over. "I found them. Hurry before they move out of sight."

Harriet toed off her trainers and stepped into the warm water. Small hermit crabs and tiny silver fish tickled her ankles and legs as they skittered away from her feet. She tried not to grimace when she sank in the fine silt.

"Belle, stay. I'll be right back." The last thing she needed was a muddy dog in the cottage. Stepping carefully so as not to lose her balance, she made her way slowly to where Martin waited.

"There's a dozen of them. Look." He pointed to the water in front of him.

Harriet moved closer. She bent down to look under the roots, but didn't see the crabs.

"I don't see them."

"I know. I lied."

Something flashed in O'Claire's hand and Harriet felt a sharp prick in the back of her neck. She immediately began to lose all feeling in her arms and legs.

Strong arms caught her. She couldn't move, but she wasn't unconscious. Terrified, she tried to speak but found she couldn't.

"You'll be fine, I promise. The paralysis is temporary."

O'Claire carried her along the edge of the swamp until he came to a skiff tied to a tree. He gently laid her on her back inside the small boat.

"This will be a little uncomfortable," he apologized. "These shallow-hulled boats tend to bounce on the water, rather than plow through the way a vee-shaped hull would, but I needed a boat that I could hide in the shallows."

Harriet could only stare at him and blink. She willed her arms to move, but it felt as if her brain had been removed from her body. She couldn't feel anything, not even her lips. This was what

Hailey must have felt like when she'd been dosed with scopolamine.

What if she stopped breathing?

O'Claire must have seen the panic in her eyes and guessed its cause.

"You'll be fine," he repeated. "I gave you a variant of Blitz that my lab worked up based on what they used to call the zombie drug. It will wear off in a few hours, once we're well away from the island with no long term effects, I promise."

Rage welled up inside Harriet. She would have screamed her frustration if she'd been able. The resort had really hit the kidnapper jackpot this week.

What did he want with her? And what did he mean, "once they were well away from the island? Where was he taking her?

Angry with William for standing her up and not wanting to be disturbed while she ran, she'd left her link on the kitchen island. How would Alex find her?

Even though she could only see sky from her position, she sensed that the skiff was moving away from the island, evidently powered by a silent motor. Waves slapped loudly at the hull, and from the corners of her eyes she saw spray fly from the bow as they gathered speed. Belle's frantic barks followed them.

Belle. She prayed the dog wouldn't try to follow them. She couldn't bear it if Belle drowned; in the short time she'd had the dog she'd become an integral part of Harriet's life.

A white wall filled Harriet's vision, the word "Bliss" written across it in blue script. The skiff bumped softly against something and she heard voices overhead. O'Claire shouted something she didn't understand.

It took her a minute to realize she was staring at the hull of the yacht she had seen offshore. Thick blue lines attached to heavy hooks snaked down the stern of the yacht. O'Claire grabbed the hooks and did something out of her field of vision. He shouted and the skiff began to rise into the air.

They were being hoisted onto the yacht's main deck.

She was in more trouble than she'd thought. Alex would never find her once O'Claire motored away from the island.

What could he possibly want with her?

She tried to think back to the various conversations they'd had over the week, but nothing stood out as a warning that O'Claire might be dangerous to her. He hadn't pried into her personal life. He'd been polite and never pushy. In short, he hadn't set off any alarm bells.

Once the skiff was settled and tied down, O'Claire lifted her in his arms once more. She tried to take in everything she could, knowing that she would have to escape as soon as she was able.

Four men dressed in white-trimmed, navy blue uniforms with holstered stun guns stood at attention. Guards. Whatever O'Claire was into, he felt the need for serious security.

"Ryan, Opie, patrol the upper deck. Tell the captain we're ready to get under way. Silas and DeShaun, I want you to patrol the main deck. I want to know if any of you see another boat, no matter how far off it is. Understood?"

The four guards disappeared from Harriet's sight. O'Claire carried her across the aft deck and down several steps. They entered a large, richly furnished salon paneled in teak. He laid her on her side on a long couch covered in deep blue leather facing a matching club chair; one that O'Claire sank into.

A pretty maid with glossy black hair to her waist appeared almost immediately. O'Claire ordered a gin and tonic. In less than a minute, he had the drink in his hand and dismissed the maid.

"I suppose you're wondering why you're here," he said, after a long sip of his drink. "You look just like your mother, you know. Except for the eyes. You have your father's eyes."

Harriet blinked in shock. This man had known her parents. O'Claire smiled.

"When you were younger you called me Uncle Mayo." He waited a beat, watching her.

Uncle Mayo. A memory surfaced, bright and clear, of a man with pewter gray eyes carrying her on his shoulders and laughing as he raced down the hill through the cult's longhouses with Danny running behind, shouting for a turn.

Martin O'Claire was Mayo Sinclair, cult leader, drug lord, and now kidnapper.

"As you can see, I did not die along with my followers. Margaret was always a little high-strung and unpredictable, but she took even me by surprise with that little incident. Fortunately for me, the Blissed cult had outlived its usefulness and it all worked out much better than I could have planned."

The man was as insane as Margaret Blackstone had been. Harriet struggled to speak, but her lips still wouldn't obey her command. She could only glare.

"I thought you died that day along with everyone else, you know." He studied Harriet's face.

"Your mother was a beautiful woman, but I think having your father's eyes adds something special to your face. You've grown into an exceptionally attractive young woman in your own right. I think I'll keep you around for a while." He sipped at his drink and looked completely relaxed.

Blink. She had to remember to blink or her eyes would dry out. She struggled to close her eyelids and would have cried out in relief when they obeyed—if only her lips would move. She tried to wiggle her fingers and toes, but nothing happened.

"I stopped to visit Margaret about six months ago," Mayo continued. "She was a loose end, you see. The law has been pushing hard to disrupt my drug business and she was the only person alive who could link me to Blitz. But when I got there it was obvious she had gone 'round the bend' as they say, and was no longer a threat. Imagine my surprise when she told me there was another surviving cult member."

Harriet stared at the man she had known as Uncle Mayo. If her memories had been intact she would have recognized him immediately. He'd had some reconstructive surgery done to alter his face–his nose was a little narrower than she remembered, his chin more squared–but she should have remembered those molten silver eyes.

"You weren't easy to track, Twinkle. By the time I traced you to Portland, you had left for the resort. It was very frustrating. I needed a way to get to you, but couldn't get a reservation on the resort until now." His cold eyes glittered with anger.

"I hate loose ends. And you are definitely a loose end."

Harriet heard a faint, deep rumble. She assumed the sound meant the yacht was getting underway, although there was no way to tell from her position on the couch. All she could see out the windows was the deck rail and blue sky with the occasional puffy white cloud. She looked back at O'Claire. He was watching her with a little smile on his face that made her heart stutter.

"I can imagine what you're thinking," he said. "How will I escape? Will I be able to swim to the island, or will we be too far away? What does the crazy preacher intend to do with me? All valid questions, but I'm afraid you'll have to wait a bit longer to learn the answers. Right now I have some business to attend to."

He emptied his glass, set it on the low brass table next to his chair, and rose. If her arms had worked she could reach out and touch him, he stood so close.

Harriet could no longer see Mayo's face, no matter how far to the left she tried to look. She gave up and stared straight ahead at his legs. With any luck, the drug he'd given her would wear off while he was away tending to his business. He hadn't bothered to tie her up, no doubt figuring his guards would catch her if she tried to escape.

She wondered how high above the water the main deck stood. Could she jump without causing herself serious injury?

The legs moved out of her sight and she sensed she was alone.

Mayo had called her by the name her parents had given her. Twinkle. A silly name, but one in keeping with the cult's customs. He never would have known of her existence if not for Margaret Blackstone. Yet another offense to be laid at that odious woman's feet.

She couldn't find any compassion in her heart for the dead chemist, especially when Blackstone continued to cause pain and heartache.

No one on the island would guess she was being held prisoner on Mayo Sinclair's yacht, which meant no one was going to come looking for her. There was no chance of rescue. She was on her own.

Hot and sudden tears filled her eyes, followed by an anger that burned away the despair that threatened. She hadn't survived two murder attempts in less than a week only to end up as shark food.

Escape was her only option.

She began to inspect the salon with her eyes, looking for anything that might help.

CHAPTER TWENTY-THREE

While she inspected the yacht's salon with her eyes, Harriet continued to try moving her hands and legs. She needed to know as soon as the drug Sinclair had injected her with began to wear off.

Deep-piled red and blue Persian rugs covered the salon floor. The large scaled, thick-armed leather furniture looked solid and well-cared for. She could smell the leather only inches from her nose—a product only the very wealthy could afford now that raising cattle for meat was strictly limited.

Evenly spaced, gleaming brass lamps provided a sharp contrast to the room's dark colors. Paper books interspersed with metal sculptures filled low bookcases that ran along the walls beneath the large windows. The room looked surprisingly comfortable and cozy.

While she took in her surroundings, she continued to fight her paralysis. Despite her efforts, she had only gained small movement in her fingers by the time Mayo returned. He reclaimed the seat he'd had before and regarded her with pursed lips. He had changed into clean khakis and a white shirt open at the neck, with the sleeves rolled to his elbows, revealing ropey, tanned forearms.

Since she still couldn't speak, she watched and waited.

"You're probably curious about the cult." Apparently restless, he stood and moved to look out the salon windows. Or was he watching to see if they were being followed?

What would Alex think when he found her trainers by the swamp? Too bad Belle couldn't tell him that she'd been abducted.

"Your parents helped me establish the Blissed."

Surprised, Harriet stopped her efforts. Payson hadn't told her that her parents were involved. Had he known they were founding members?

Mayo looked over his shoulder at her. "Your father and I were close friends at university. We played basketball together, roomed together, and we both wanted to date your mother, but she only had eyes for James."

James. Her father's name had been James before he changed it to Arcturus. Harriet took the nugget of information and held it close. It was the first time she'd heard her father's real name used. Her aunt refused to speak of him—she blamed Harriet's father for the untimely death of her mother, even though he had died at the same time.

"We were naïve idealists back then, of course. We were going to change the world; create a community that would live in harmony with nature and each other. Live off the land. Provide for ourselves without the use of technology." His voice dripped with disgust.

"We were nothing more than beggars—migrant farm hands going where we could find work picking crops for the landowners—until I met Margaret Blackstone. She was a lonely lab nerd, desperate for male attention and I was only too happy to give it to her once I learned that she was rich and easily manipulated. It didn't take long to persuade her to invest in our cause and buy the land in Apple Valley."

Harriet sent up a silent prayer of thanks that her mother had chosen her father over the selfish egomaniac standing at the window.

Without being obvious about it, she resumed her efforts to move; testing her muscles. Her fingers and toes responded to her efforts but her arms and legs were still frozen.

"It was a good set-up, what we had." Mayo frowned at her. Harriet stilled and waited until he returned his attention to whatever he was watching out the window.

"I made it clear to Margaret that I needed a variety of women and she agreed as she didn't want to lose me. Building the compound and the Blissed membership entertained me for a few years, but eventually I realized I didn't want to be stuck in the backwoods forever. I wanted more. I wanted power and that requires money–more money than Margaret had. Certainly more money than our fresh food and handmade crafts brought in the nearest town.

Moving away from the window, Mayo took his earlier seat. He stretched out his long legs and crossed them at the ankles.

"I needed a new gig–one that would bring in large amounts of cash–so I asked Margaret to create a drug that would make users feel great and be addictive. Once I got them hooked, then I'd have a steady and guaranteed income stream. She came up with Blitz and I knew I had a moneymaker. Unfortunately, not all of the cult members were happy about becoming dealers–your parents included."

Harriet was glad to hear that her parents had wanted nothing to do with the drug that had destroyed so many lives and families.

"Then Penny came along and things changed. I knew Douglas Wade was Penny's brother because she introduced us once."

Mayo's silver eyes glittered. "She provided an opportunity to tap a vast, unbelievable amount of wealth, but Margaret's jealousy became a problem before I could devise a plan to access it."

The man had never cared about anyone in the cult. He was a cold-blooded user of his friends and followers. Like most self-centered people, Harriet knew Mayo considered himself the hero of his story and the only important character.

"Margaret immediately took a dislike against Penny and became more and more of a nuisance. Then one of my dealers got careless and was arrested. The idiot told them he got the drugs from the Blissed Cult in an ill-conceived attempt to save himself a prison sentence. I needed to disappear, but I had a problem. The cult members all knew that I was responsible for the drug. I eliminated the ones who'd been acting as my dealers, but I still had too many witnesses."

He snapped his fingers. "And just like that, Margaret took care of my problem and I didn't have to lift a finger. I slipped away in the chaos and reinvented myself. New name. New face. Set up a new lab. Anticipating a possible falling out, I had stolen the formula for Blitz from Margaret early on. Frankly there was too much money to be made to quit the drug business. So I became a legitimate businessman and sometimes preacher named Martin O'Claire and funneled the drug money through my companies."

Leaning forward, Mayo's eyes bore into Harriet's own. "Everything worked out–until I went to see Margaret and she told me you were still alive. Imagine my shock. How much did eight year old you know and how much did you remember? Were you a threat? I couldn't take the chance. Like I said before, you are my last loose end."

Harriet forced herself to hold her gaze steady. Mayo scared the crap out of her, but she knew it was a mistake to let him know that. He was a man who preyed on the weak. He would only respect strength.

Mayo's link buzzed. He answered it, his eyes now hooded but still staring at her while he listened to whoever was on the other end. When he ended the call, he drummed his fingers on the arm of the chair.

"I have some business to attend to." He checked his wrist unit. "The drug should begin wearing off in the next half hour or so. Please don't leave the salon. You cannot escape the ship; my guards will stop you. Feel free to pour yourself a drink. The bar's against the wall behind you. I shouldn't be long. When I return you can tell me about your life after your parents died."

So. He didn't plan to kill her immediately. If he simply wanted her dead, he could have killed her at the swamp and left her body for the saltwater crocs. There would've been nothing left but her trainers after the crocs dragged her body deeper into the swamp where they could feast in peace.

Be grateful for small blessings, her aunt used to tell her.

When was a blessing not a blessing? Harriet closed her eyes and focused on moving her fingers.

CHAPTER TWENTY-FOUR

"Solly, have you seen or talked with Harriet in the last few hours?" Alex paced Mermaid Cottage's living room and tried to rein in his worry.

Surprise registered on Solly's face, giving him his answer.

"I thought you were looking after her." Someone spoke in the background. Solly looked away, said a few words, then turned back to face Alex.

"How could you lose her with kidnappers on the loose?"

"Turns out Rodney Lynch and Angela Daly were our kidnappers–"

"Wait. I thought Angela was kidnapped," Solly interrupted.

"They were in it together, then Angela murdered Rodney. I've just come from wrapping up the interview with her and Fox, and Harriet is missing. She stayed for the interview for a bit, but decided to head home. The Hog is here. She and Belle are missing."

"I'm on my way." Solly cut the call before Alex could ask him to check the south end of the beach.

He'd come home after making arrangements for Angela to be met on the mainland and taken into custody, expecting to find

Harriet either on the lanai with a glass of wine or sound asleep in their bed.

She'd been running on fumes for days now—never getting enough sleep and not her usual energetic self during the day. Usually in good spirits, she'd been jumpy and unusually quiet since returning to the island. Lord knew she had good reason, but it still concerned him.

Two attempts on her life in the past week was more than any sane person could handle, let alone someone who was already emotionally stretched to the breaking point.

Margaret Blackstone had tried to poison Harriet and cover it up with a fire. The next day a guest tried to overdose her with scopolamine when Harriet caught the guest in the act of trying to kill the guest's cousin. Harriet shook it off and returned to work, but then the first kidnapping happened.

It had definitely been the week from hell as far as Harriet was concerned.

He hadn't helped any by asking her to marry him. He mentally kicked himself for being an insensitive clod. Way to lay on the emotional pressure. Would it have hurt him to wait a few weeks, until she settled in to her new memories?

Now he had to wait anyway. What if Harriet never asked him to marry her? He didn't know what he'd do. She was The One. Even when he thought she might be a murderer, he'd been irresistably drawn to her.

Alex groaned. He might have made a mistake handing Harriet the power over their future. He was so used to always being in control–

He pushed away the uneasiness and concentrated on the immediate problem. Where was Harriet?

The Hog sat outside the cottage, which meant she had to be nearby. He went to the coat hooks and shoes neatly lined up beside the back door and saw an empty space where her trainers should be.

"Dammit." She shouldn't be out on her own. Not in the fragile state she was in.

He headed to the lanai to check the beach. A few people walked along the water's edge; none of them Harriet. In the distance, a large yacht moved toward the horizon. He'd noticed the yacht anchored off the island earlier that morning and meant to ask Payson who it belonged to. The resort monitored all boats within a nautical mile radius of the resort. But the day's events had pushed the yacht from his mind.

"Alex. Have you heard from her?" Solly rounded the corner of the cottage and stepped onto the lanai.

"No. Her trainers are gone. She must have taken Belle for a run."

Solly gazed down the beach the same way Alex had. "How long has she been gone?"

"I don't know. According to the cottage's alarm, she reset it close to two hours ago. I expected her to be home well before now."

"Have you tried tracking her link?"

"She left it here, in the kitchen." He huffed and exasperated sigh. "She's supposed to keep it with her at all times."

"Have you checked her messages?"

"No messages. Her call log shows one from William not long after she left the hotel."

Solly's brows shot up in surprise. "Why did William call her?"

"I have no idea."

"Huh. We might as well take a run. We'll probably meet her on the beach."

"Agreed. Meet here in five." Both men went to change into running gear. Alex reset the cottage's alarm and they took off at a brisk pace.

"Those are Harriet's tracks," Alex said, pointing to the footprints they were following. "I recognize the pattern of her trainers."

"It looks like she had company."

"Yeah. Male company. They're larger and deeper. William, maybe?" The two sets of tracks stretched in front of them as far as he could see.

Solly laughed. "Definitely not William. The man doesn't do exercise. Something I intend to address. Who else would she be running with? You were with Fox, right? There's no one else."

When the swamp came into view they saw Belle on the water's edge.

Alex picked up his pace. Harriet would never leave Belle on her own at the swamp. She was obsessed with doing right by the gentle beast.

"Belle!" Alex approached the dog, but she continued to pace the water's edge and paid him no attention.

"Alex! Harry's trainers!" Solly held up a pair of familiar trainers.

For a brief moment, Alex couldn't draw a full breath. What had happened there?

"Do you see any blood?" He could barely get the question out, his throat was so tight.

"No. No blood." The two men looked at each other with relief. "Why would she take off her trainers?" Solly asked.

"To wade in the water, maybe? I don't know. But there aren't any tracks headed back."

He looked at Belle, who continued to pace the shore, and frowned at the yacht motoring away from the island. "We have to get back to the cottage."

"We aren't going to search the swamp?"

"See that yacht out there? Belle hasn't taken her eyes off it. I have a feeling our girl has been kidnapped."

"That's–" Solly stopped. He knew Alex was a brilliant ex-detective. If his gut told him Harry was on the yacht, then she was probably on the yacht.

"What about Belle? We can't just leave her here."

"We have no choice. She isn't going to follow us until we find Harriet. Let's go."

William was standing outside Venus Cottage when they arrived; both short of breath from running full out. Solly gave him a brief kiss. Before Alex could ask if William had seen anything, Solly told him Harriet was missing.

"I know."

That stopped both men in their tracks. William flinched when Alex grabbed his upper arm. Harriet had been trying to tell him that something was going on with the pastry chef, but he hadn't really paid attention because he didn't think it was any of her business. It was damn well his business now.

"What do you know?" He tightened his grip. "Speak before I really hurt you."

William's eyes darted to Solly, who stared at him in disbelief, and licked his lips.

"It's my half-brother. He found out Harriet was alive and on the island."

Solly frowned. "Why would he think Harriet was dead? And more importantly, why would he care?"

"Because he assumed she had died along with the other cult members," William answered. "Then he visited his old girlfriend and learned that Harriet had survived. He became obsessed with finding her."

"He traced her to the resort." Alex's tone was flat.

William nodded and tried to pull his arm away with no success.

"What's your role in this?" Alex demanded.

A deep flush crept over William's face. Staring at his feet, he mumbled something. Alex released his arm suddenly and grabbed him by his neck under his round jaw.

"Tell me, or I swear I'll snap your neck."

"I had no choice," he pleaded, staring at Solly. "You have to believe me, I had no choice. He would have hurt or killed me if I didn't do what he asked. He's a bully."

"What did he ask of you, Will?" Solly asked softly.

"He just wanted me to keep an eye on Harry. Tell him her routine. Let him know when she was alone."

He struggled to swallow past Alex's fingers digging into his neck. "He-he had me tag her and ask her to meet me here. I didn't hurt her or anything," he hurried to add. "I promise."

Alex released William's neck with a violent shove. William went sprawling in the sand.

"Name. I want a name."

"Mayo Sinclair. He goes by Martin O'Claire now."

Solly looked at Alex. "Does the name Mayo Sinclair mean something to you?"

"Yeah. He's the guy who started the Blissed cult. The cult where Harriet lived the first eight years of her life," he explained, when he saw Solly's puzzled expression. He hadn't realized how estranged the two friends had become in the past week. Solly didn't know that Harriet had regained some of her memories.

"Mayo was also responsible for the manufacturing and sale of Blitz."

"He still is," William said from where he still lay in the sand.

Alex's gaze sharpened. "Tell me." He reached down and pulled William to his feet.

"Mayo is very careful. He set up a series of small labs around the world and funnels the money from drug sales though his businesses. No one connects Martin O'Claire to cult leader Mayo Sinclair, who has been missing and forgotten for nearly twenty years. When he found out Harriet survived, he knew he had to find her. Harriet's the only one who can identify him."

"So you're saying this Mayo dude is going to kill Harry?" Solly looked horrified.

"He won't kill her right away. Mayo has a colossal ego. He'll want to know what she remembers about the cult and him. He'll keep her alive for a while."

"You're wrong about one thing," Alex said. "Harriet isn't the only one who can identify Mayo Sinclair. So can his half brother."

CHAPTER TWENTY-FIVE

The next time Mayo returned, Harriet was sitting up on the couch. She had tried to stand and leave the salon, but her legs were still too wobbly to support her. She managed to cross them as she sat back, doing her best to look in control, calm and collected.

"Ah. I see you're regaining control of your body. Good. I told you the paralysis wouldn't be permanent. Now we can have a proper conversation."

"Why am I here?" Harriet spoke slowly. It took effort to enunciate clearly. How long would it take for the drug to clear her body?

"Are you planning to kill me?"

"Possibly. Once I tire of you. That should be incentive to be as entertaining as you can."

Harriet gave him an incredulous look. "Entertain you? You're insane, you know that? I'm glad my mother chose James over you. I would hate for you to be my father."

"If your mother had chosen me, you never would've been born. I made sure early on that I wouldn't add to the world's population." He snapped his fingers and the maid reappeared.

Harriet wondered if her only duty was to stand at attention just outside the door the way a droid would. A moment later, Mayo held a bubbling drink filled with round ice cubes.

"I imagine your boyfriend the ex-detective will be looking for you soon. He seems very capable, but don't get your hopes up. We're well away from the island and the odds are slim that anyone would ever guess that you're on board my yacht."

"Won't the resort notice that they're one guest short when they check everyone for the trip back to the mainland?"

Mayo shrugged. "It won't matter. By then we'll have transferred to my second yacht and we'll be well on our way to Venezuela. Martin O'Claire and his hostage Harriet Monroe will be thought lost at sea when they find the wreckage of the *Blissed* floating in the ocean."

He was going to destroy the yacht? It wasn't until it snuffed out like a candle flame that Harriet realized she'd been holding onto a slim hope of rescue.

"I never recognized you, you know. If you had ignored me at the resort you never would've even come up on my radar," she told him. "You could have left the resort without me ever being the wiser."

Mayo took a thoughtful sip of his drink. Harriet would have liked one herself, but she wasn't sure she could hold a glass without shaking, so she didn't ask.

"The day I approached you when you were looking for the first kidnapped guest, I was testing you to see if you recognized me. But when you didn't know me, it bugged me. I found I wanted you to remember, so I 'bumped' into you as often as I could. You're very like your mother, you know. Beautiful, charming, intelligent. A genuinely nice person."

Harriet didn't like what she saw in his eyes. "But I'm not my mother. You can't think to replace her with me."

Mayo said nothing; merely sipped at his drink.

"How long before we meet up with the other yacht?"

"A few hours yet. I want to do the transfer after dark in case any satellites overhead are watching."

"How do you know William? I heard you arguing with him earlier today."

"He's my younger half brother. Same mother, different fathers."

"He's been helping you, hasn't he?"

"Some. He kept an eye on you for me. Oh, he tried to resist," Mayo said, after seeing Harriet's expression. "He knew Solly wouldn't like it. He does care about your friend. The problem is that our Willy Boy is a bit of a pansy. I've always been able to make him do what I want. One just has to know how to apply the right pressure. That's true with everybody, of course."

"You're a bully."

Mayo shrugged and looked unconcerned. "Call it what you want. I get things done, and done my way."

"Aren't you worried about William turning you in? Reporting you to the authorities? Even after you kill me, there'll still be someone who can identify you. Will you kill him too?"

"I can control William. Besides, our mother would be upset if anything happened to him."

Harriet closed her eyes. She felt exhausted. She didn't want to talk; she wanted to think and plan. She wanted Mayo to go away. Unfortunately he had other ideas.

"Tell me what happened to you after your parents died."

"After my parents were murdered you mean." He inclined his head in acknowledgement.

"I went to live with my aunt and uncle in Portland."

"But you didn't stay. You were only fifteen when you left them. Why?"

Harriet wasn't about to go into her reasons for why she ran away with her kidnapper. Fortunately one of the guards entered the salon. Silas or DeShaun—she didn't know which, just that he was one of the two told to patrol the main deck.

"Speedboat approaching from the island, Boss."

"Tell the captain to increase our speed and then stay out of sight. Tell DeShaun. They'll be forced to turn back when they can't board. If they persist in following us, they'll run out of fuel well before we rendezvous with the *Starlight*."

Silas nodded and left to do as ordered. Mayo scratched his nose and looked bored.

"They'll report you, you know. You won't get away."

"Either your boyfriend made a lucky guess or my idiot half brother talked. Either way it doesn't matter, so don't get your hopes up—although I will punish William when I see him next." The sound of his strong teeth cracking on ice sounded loud in the quiet salon.

"We'll make the rendezvous, never fear. Once the *Bliss* blows, the sharks will come and take care of enough body parts to make any would-be rescuers believe we blew up with the ship and were devoured. A tidy disappearance, if I do say so myself."

"Did you really see Patricia Williams in the hotel lobby the morning she disappeared?"

"No. I needed a reason to speak with you and introduce myself. But thanks for reminding me. There's something I need to deal with."

"Victoria, have Ryan and Opie report to the salon." He watched Harriet in silence until the two guards arrived. It took all her willpower not to squirm or speak, but she managed.

"Opie, relieve Ryan of his weapon."

Opie looked surprised, but did as told. Ryan paled beneath his tan and looked nervous.

"I believe you lost something of mine," Mayo told him.

"I don't know how it happened, Boss. Honest. I–"

"Enough. I went to a great deal of trouble and expensive

bribes to steal that decoder. You were supposed to take possession of it and bring it straight to me. You were careless, and you know how I feel about careless help."

Beads of sweat appeared on Ryan's brow. "I'll make it up to you, Boss, I swear."

Mayo looked bored. "Your instructions were to pick up the decoder and return to the yacht. Did you follow my instructions?"

"I knew we weren't leaving the dock until the next morning," Ryan said defensively. "I wanted to see Angie before we left."

"You wanted to see Angie." Mayo heaved a sigh. "You've always had a weakness for licensed companions, Rye, and one in particular. She is pretty, I'll give you that."

His eyes turned a stormy gray that reminded Harriet of the New England sky right before a hurricane. They sent a shiver down her spine.

"Your weakness for licensed companions makes you vulnerable. And if you're vulnerable, I'm vulnerable. You bragged to her about the decoder, didn't you?"

Ryan's throat convulsed. "I-I might have said something."

Harriet's eyes widened in surprise. Mayo was behind the theft of the decoder and his guard Ryan was the customer Angela Daly had stolen the decoder from. Why hadn't Mayo realized it was missing before now?

"I trusted you to do your job, Ryan. Imagine my surprise when I returned to the yacht today and checked the briefcase—only to found it empty." He shoved up from his chair and got in Ryan's face, his voice quiet. Ryan paled even more.

"I saw your precious Angie on the island with her friend. Women were being kidnapped, Ryan. Did you know that? I wondered how a kidnapper managed to access the hotel's locked rooms. Now I know. Your precious Angie stole the decoder, didn't she?"

He didn't realize that Angela had been found out and the decoder returned to Payson.

"How do you think I feel about that?"

"I'll get it back, Boss." Ryan's adam's apple bobbed up and down nervously.

"Too late. Opie. Take care of Ryan."

In a flash, Opie had Ryan's hands secured behind him with a zip-tie. He marched Ryan from the salon. A long minute later, Harriet heard a yell.

"What—what did he do with him?" She wasn't sure she wanted to know, but she had to ask.

"Tossed him off the stern."

Ryan would drown within minutes with his hands secured behind him. Harriet tried not to think about the man struggling to stay afloat.

Mayo watched her with hooded eyes. She could sense him stewing over the lost decoder. How much money had he wasted on bribes? How did he even find the right person to bribe? She knew Payson would be asking the same questions.

After a few minutes, he turned away and left the salon. Harriet pushed the thought of the drowning man away and focused on her own plight.

He'd named the second yacht after her mother. Starlight was the name her mother took when they created the cult. Mayo Sinclair may have taken many lovers, but it was obvious to Harriet that he never got over losing her mother to his friend James.

It was probably why he hadn't simply tossed her off the stern—yet. Harriet had a feeling that Mayo wouldn't keep her around for long once he truly understood that she was not her mother.

Her gaze was drawn to the windows. It would be dark soon. The red ball of the sun hung low above the horizon. She pushed to her feet, using the arm of the couch to help her stand upright, and took a few shaky steps. She needed to be ready to take advantage of even the smallest opportunity for escape.

As she slowly paced the salon, the strength began to return to her thighs and calves. No matter how strong she felt, once it was dark she'd make a bid for freedom. She'd have to leap over the side of the yacht.

Then she remembered about the sharks. Mayo had said they would show up after the explosion to feast on body parts. Whose body parts? Was he planning to sacrifice the yacht's crew?

There would be another crew aboard the *Starlight*. Blowing up the crew along with the *Bliss* would make anyone looking for her believe she was dead. More proof that people were nothing more than expendable tools to Mayo.

It was time to check out the main deck. She opened the salon door and found Silas leaning against the starboard deck rail.

"You aren't allowed to move around the ship," he said, standing up.

"I-I feel sick to my stomach. I need fresh air. I'll just walk to the stern and back. I promise." She sounded weak and like she was begging. That wouldn't do. Harriet straightened her shoulders.

"Look, I'm going to be ill all over the place if I have to stay in there. I need to stretch my legs and get some air. I'm going to walk around the deck. Don't worry–I won't jump. I can't swim and I'm afraid of sharks." She headed down the deck alongside the salon without waiting for an answer.

Halfway to the stern she stopped, grabbed the rail, and looked out to the horizon. Without turning her head, she checked on Silas. He stood watching her, but hadn't followed her.

Good.

She scanned for the motorboat that Silas had reported earlier but there wasn't another craft in sight. That Alex had been forced to give up didn't surprise her. The resort's motorboats had a range limited to the amount of fuel they carried. They were built for short excursions and speed, not distance.

She estimated the distance to the water at around thirty feet. The Olympic high dive for women ranged from fifty-nine to seventy-five feet. She could survive the drop even if she hit badly, but she would hurt herself. She'd have to try to drop straight in.

Surprisingly enough for a city girl, she could swim and was comfortable in the water. What freaked her out were all the creatures who lived beneath its surface. She knew sharks didn't particularly like human flesh, but all it took was one testing bite to make a body bleed out.

Scanning the water beneath her, she saw nothing to alarm her. She would wait for the sun to set and take her chances.

Once the sun touched the horizon, it seemed to speed up its descent. In far too short a time there was only a tiny red sliver left, and then that disappeared as well. Stars sparkled in the deep indigo sky. The moon was slightly past full and wouldn't rise until later.

Still she waited. The throbbing beneath her bare feet decreased slightly. She became aware of another low thrumming. She scanned the horizon but at first saw nothing. Then a bulky shadow crossed the yacht's bow and blotted out a few low-hanging stars. She realized Mayo's second yacht had been steadily approaching from the opposite side of the ship. If she'd chosen the port side to walk she would have seen it earlier.

Behind her, the yacht's lights went out.

She glanced back. Silas was still watching her, although he had relaxed and leaned against the rail again. The bitter smell of his cigarette reached her.

It was time. She braced herself and took a deep breath.

"Harriet." The whisper sounded from beyond the salon. Surprised, Harriet turned toward the sound but saw no one.

"Harriet. This way. Quickly."

Harriet glanced back at Silas, then began to walk slowly aft. When she drew level with the aft wall of the salon, the voice spoke again.

"Keep walking. When you reach the stern, run to the port side, away from Silas, and jump off the side of the ship. Don't jump off the stern or you'll get caught up in the screws. I'll be right behind you."

The speaker was female. The only woman Harriet had seen was the maid in the salon who made Mayo's drinks.

The thought that she might have an ally on board the yacht buoyed her spirits, although the knowledge that she had to leap into the ocean still frightened her.

Harriet cleared the salon and turned toward the port side of the boat. She immediately bumped into something and stumbled.

"Watch out for the deck chairs," the voice hissed. "Hurry. We haven't much time."

Victoria's petite figure emerged from the dark shadows, dragging something behind her. Silas shouted Harriet's name.

"Run. Jump. Go!"

Harriet ran for the port rail, crashing into several more deck chairs which slowed her down. Despite her load, Victoria reached the rail ahead of her. The yacht's engines faded to a faint hum and it noticeably slowed.

"Hurry!" Victoria lifted the object to the top of the rail, fiddled with it for a moment, and pushed it over. A beam of light lit the port walkway.

Harriet cleared the deck chair obstacle course and raced to the rail. Victoria already balanced atop it. The beam picked out her dark hair blowing in the light breeze, and then she was gone.

With her heart in her throat, Harriet heaved her body over the rail.

CHAPTER TWENTY-SIX

It took a lifetime to reach the water.

Despite that, Harriet didn't have time to right herself and hit the hard surface fanny first. It slapped hard against the back of her bare legs and wedged her shorts.

She remembered to plug her nose seconds before she went under. The water was much cooler than the water off the beach. The shock helped clear her head of any lingering effects from the drug Mayo had given her.

The upper world shut off when the water closed over her head. She was in complete darkness with only the sound of the yachts' screws and her beating heart to break the sudden silence. Darkness surrounded her, providing no clue as to which way she should swim.

Panic coursed through her body. She needed air, but which direction was up?

When she was eighteen, she and Solly hitchhiked to Pine Point Beach to get away from the city's summer heat. They'd had a great time, right up until a large wave crashed into Harriet and knocked her under, tossing her about like a piece of flotsam. She swam for the surface and hit the sandy bottom instead. She had panicked then, convinced that she was about to drown.

As soon as she stopped fighting, the natural buoyancy of her body had begun to carry her to the surface. At least there had been sunshine then. Now there was only an inky blackness.

She forced herself to go lax and waited. After a long minute, she felt herself begin to rise. Now that she had a direction, she struck out for the surface with everything she had left.

Sparks of light began to flash in her eyes and she knew she wasn't going to make it. Her lungs rebelled until she was forced to expel small amounts of air. With her last bit of breath, she kicked as hard and fast as she could and broke free with a loud sob. Gulping noisily, she sucked in the night air as fast as her lungs would cooperate.

"Quiet."

Thank god. Victoria was nearby.

Something dark loomed behind the maid, making Harriet's heart stutter until she realized it wasn't alive. It bobbed on the water, following Victoria as she swam closer to Harriet.

"Get in the raft. Hurry. We don't have much time."

A raft. Harriet wanted to weep with joy, but it would have to wait. Mayo would be sending his guards after them any moment now. She swam the few strokes to the raft. Grabbing its side, she hoisted herself out of the water and fell in. Victoria immediately joined her.

The bottom felt flimsy and held several inches of water, but as far as Harriet was concerned, it was perfect.

"Grab the other oar and start paddling."

Harriet did as told. She had questions, but they could wait until they'd escaped the yacht. She pulled the small oar from its bungee straps, kneeled next to the edge of the raft, and began to paddle.

Water sloshed around her knees and she was shivering, but it didn't matter. She wasn't going to end up in Venezuela.

The women paddled hard for ten minutes, putting some distance between them and the *Bliss* before taking a breather.

"Thank you," Harriet said. "I was planning to jump, but I'm sure I would've ended up as fish food without your help."

"We aren't out of the woods yet. The *Bliss* is going to blow in another few minutes. The farther away we are, the better our chance of surviving the blast."

Harriet dug in with her paddle until her hands blistered and her arms and shoulder muscles burned.

"Why aren't they coming after us?" She had expected Mayo to launch the flat-bottomed skiff he'd used to abduct her and race after them, but there was no sign of activity on the dark yacht.

Her companion said nothing. Harriet could barely make out Victoria's face in the starlight. She had stopped paddling and was staring back at the yacht, waiting.

Harriet turned around just as a deep boom sounded. A heavy wall of heated air hit the raft. A bright fireball split the yacht, sending bits and pieces high into the air. Burning debris fell around them, hissing when it hit the water.

"Paddle!" Victoria shouted. "We're too close. If one of those burning pieces hit the raft it will melt through."

Harriet turned away from the spectacle and pushed her aching muscles to work again. Two more booms clapped across the water.

Stunned, Harriet stopped paddling and turned to look at the burning yacht. The second and third explosion had finished the job, breaking it into smaller pieces that burned until they sank beneath the surface. They lit up the area, reflected off the water, and illuminated Victoria's smiling face.

Lights appeared on the *Starlight*. Was Mayo aboard?

"No."

Harriet hadn't realized she'd spoken aloud. She resumed her paddling.

"Who are you?"

"Victoria Simms. I've been working undercover for the last year with the DEA."

The Drug Enforcement Agency?

"You've been undercover for a year?" Harriet considered what that meant. No contact with friends or family. Living under the constant threat of discovery. She couldn't imagine anything more stressful.

"You look like you're about fifteen."

"I'm thirty-four. People tend to underestimate the young."

"Including Mayo?"

"Definitely including Mayo. Watch out!" A piece of burning fiberglass hull landed in the water next to Harriet with a hiss and a splash. To her surprise, it continued to burn, releasing a noxious, bitter odor.

They maneuvered the raft away from the debris and kept paddling. Neither woman spoke. Harriet was working something out in her head.

"You blew up the *Bliss*, didn't you?"

Victoria remained silent for so long, Harriet didn't think she was going to answer.

"Mayo's labs are being seized and demolished as we speak. The Starlight will be intercepted and dealt with. One of the worst drug scourges the planet has ever known has been eradicated."

"And Mayo? His guards?"

"Mayo got a taste of his own product. As did the guards. Keep paddling."

Harriet knew that was all she would get out of her companion. Had Victoria doctored Mayo's drink with the same stuff he'd used on her? She pictured him lying on the yacht, unable to move, but aware of everything.

She guessed it was enough. She had her answer. She didn't know how Victoria had managed it–nor did she want to know the details–but she knew that Mayo and everyone on the *Bliss* had died in the blast.

When the Blitz currently on the streets dried up there would be no more. Addicts would suffer terribly, but no new addicts would be created. It wasn't the way the justice system was supposed to work, but maybe it was for the best. As long as Mayo lived there would be fresh supplies of Blitz. And who knew how he intended to use the drug that had incapacitated her?

Harriet didn't bother asking any more questions. It took all of her will power to keep plying the paddle in the water. Her world shrank to one thought. Stroke. Stroke. The pain between her shoulder blades intensified until it felt as if she'd been stuck with a hot poker, and still they paddled on through the night.

The half moon rose, creating a shimmery path of moonlight on the water's surface. Harriet had no idea where they were headed. Would someone come looking for them? Surely the explosion had been seen–either by a boat in the distance or a passing satellite.

Her reserves had been sorely depleted over the last week and she was running on empty. She barely had the strength to lift the paddle again, let alone pull it through the resisting water. She let it fall into the raft and leaned against the inflated side.

It would be dawn soon. Wasn't it always darkest before the dawn?

Why hadn't she said yes when Alex asked her to marry him? If she didn't make it, would that be the last memory he held of her? The thought made her want to weep. He deserved so much better. If she survived, the very first thing she needed to do was ask Alex to marry her.

CHAPTER TWENTY-SEVEN

Two Weeks Later

"Where's the bride?"

Harriet's heart nearly burst with love. She stood at the far end of the aisle created by their wedding guests. The entire resort staff and nearly two hundred young orphans dressed in fancy new dresses beamed at her and whispered excitedly to one another.

At the opposite end of the aisle in front of a magnificent arbor covered in pale rose and white roses, stood the most important people in her life. She could see the shine in Solly's eyes from where she stood.

Tarbell smiled at her, and Alex–Alex's face was filled with love and satisfaction. Behind them, the sea sparkled and white gulls wheeled in the air as if in celebration of what was about to take place.

"Are you ready, my dear?" Payson held out his arm and Harriet took it. He had eschewed his regular island wear for a fitted white suit with a pale rose-colored shirt and pocket hankie. She had made him take off his tie. Today was a day to relax and have fun. Ties were not allowed.

He placed his other hand over hers and gave it a squeeze.

"Thank you for inviting me to be a part of this."

"You're my family. There's no one else I would rather walk down the aisle with." She hoped if her parents were watching from heaven that her father would forgive her.

"Penny would have loved this. Everything you've done."

"*We've* done," Harriet corrected him, squeezing his arm. Apparently she wasn't the only one thinking of the dearly departed.

She herself was barefoot. Her slim, rose-colored sheath skimmed her body, ending just above the knee. She carried a small bouquet of white rosebuds that Solly had handed her while the guests were assembling.

"I love you," he'd told her, pressing the bouquet into her hands. "I couldn't be happier for you both."

She'd pulled him in for a fierce hug. "I love you, too. Thank you for being my man of honor."

After a long talk, they had repaired their friendship. Solly had tried to apologize for not giving weight to her suspicions about William, but she wouldn't let him. William had moved out of Solly's cottage but still baked for the resort. Harriet was hoping they would reconcile. They were good together, and now that Mayo Sinclair could no longer threaten his half-brother, Harriet had seen William's confidence grow.

Tarbell Fox stood next to Alex, a silly grin on his face. His girlfriend, Tamara, had returned to the island with the circus a week earlier. Harriet was touched that the circus folk cared enough to interrupt their tour on such short notice. They would be leaving again to finish their European tour after the wedding, but Tamara was staying behind.

Harriet thought the resort might be celebrating another wedding soon, given the way and and Tarbell couldn't stop smiling at each other.

"Mizz Mun-row, shouldn't you be walking down the aisle now?" Hayley, one of the orphans Harriet had grown close to, stood on the edge of the guests and pointed toward the arbor.

"They're waiting, you know."

Harriet grinned. "So they are. It must be time."

Satisfied that she'd moved the ceremony along, Hayley beamed.

"Here comes the bride," she yelled. There were chuckles and faces turned in anticipation. Harriet's stomach tightened in response. She took a deep breath and started forward with Payson matching her steps.

She managed to get through her vows without stumbling. Albie, the head luggage handler at the hotel and an ordained minister, turned his dark face to Alex.

"Alex Hayes, do you take this woman to be your lawfully wedded wife? To have and to hold, in sickness and in health, until death do you part?"

Alex turned his deep blue eyes to Harriet.

"I didn't want to love you. Loving means opening myself to pain and loss again. But I can't imagine my life without you in it, so I have to reconcile the two. As a wise man once said, 'It's better to have loved and lost, then never to have loved at all.' And I do love you, with all my heart, with all that I am."

Harriet's eyes filled with tears. Alex turned back to Albie.

"I certainly do, Albie. Now pronounce us man and wife so I can kiss my bride."

Harriet's escape and the consequent destruction of the *Bliss* had faded to a surreal memory. Despite Payson sending out a search party, the raft had been spotted by a sailboat around mid morning the following day, and Victoria and Harriet brought onboard. The family of sailors had altered their course and contacted the island.

Payson dispatched a helicopter to meet them and take them to the mainland hospital where they were met by men in dark suits and separated.

She never saw Victoria–if that was the woman's real name–again. She was interviewed by the suits and signed an agreement never to disclose what happened on the *Bliss* after it was put to her that anything she said could endanger their undercover agent. Within twenty-four hours she'd been discharged and returned to the resort.

Alex met the shuttle when Captain Rod landed. Much to her relief, Rod had managed to clean and eliminate the awful odors left by Angela and Rodney's kidnap victims in Payson's private shuttle. Angela sat in a mainland prison, awaiting trial for the murder of her friend. Rodney's body had been released to his family for cremation.

Upon seeing Alex waiting for her, Harriet wasted no time. She knew what she wanted. What she needed. Everything else would work itself out.

"Will you marry me?" He opened his arms and she stepped in, secure in the knowledge that this was the man she was meant to spend her life with.

And now here they were, celebrating their union with all the people who mattered. After the vows, everyone cheered and the real celebration began.

Upon her return, Payson had met with the resort employees to inform them of major changes to be put into effect immediately.

Children were now the resort's priority. Each group of orphans would stay in the hotel for the first three weeks of every month. The fourth week was now set aside for the employees to rest and prepare for the next influx of guests.

Besides the orphans, the cottages on the four pirate coves would be earmarked for families with sick or disabled children. The resort was in the process of changing its status to a non-profit entity. Harriet was busy putting together programs for the children and soliciting sponsors.

Art and theatre classes were being developed, a variety of instructors for the special-needs children brought in, and everyone would be encouraged to use all the resort had to offer. Much to her delight, the circus had offered to train anyone interested in their acts. Harriet had so many ideas she could barely sleep. Even Payson was fired up about their new direction.

They'd kicked off the new format by inviting all the orphans who'd been to the island previously to the wedding. She'd been afraid that it would be a lonely affair, since Alex had no family left and she only had Solly and Payson, but the wedding turned into a large, glorious gathering.

After the brief ceremony, a surprisingly talented group of resort employees began to play live music. The island music was better than anything prerecorded that Harriet might have chosen. Employees danced and ate and drank. The orphans whirled and chased each other in their pretty frocks and laughed. Their laughter made the day.

Everywhere she looked, Harriet saw smiling faces. She noticed Payson standing off to one side beneath a trio of palm trees. A woman approached him. Slim and white-haired, she wore a wide smile.

Harriet saw the shock on Payson's face before he started forward. He stopped when they drew close, but the woman held out her arms. Payson looked at her for a long moment, then stepped forward and wrapped his arms around her.

"Who is that with Payson?"

Harriet watched them walk away from the party, arms wrapped around each other's waists, before turning to Alex.

"*That* is Stella Wade, the love of Payson's life. I tracked her down and invited her to the wedding. She was only too happy to accept."

"Good for you. Payson deserves someone special."

Alex's voice deepened and grew husky. "Hello, Mrs. Hayes." An arm snaked around Harriet's waist and pulled her close. She leaned her head on her husband's shoulder.

"Hello, husband." The word felt good and right.

"Have you seen the cake William made yet?" Alex asked. He nuzzled her hair. "They just carried it out."

"No." Harriet leaned back to look around Alex. The largest cake she'd ever seen sat in the middle of the tables bearing food.

"Wow. How many tiers it that?"

"I think I counted twelve. Fox said William was a wreck worrying about moving it."

"It's absolutely beautiful." The palest cream icing covered the twelve layers. Rose and white roses anchored the bottom of each layer in alternating bands of color. A couple in island dress topped the incredible confection.

"Can we have cake now?" One of the orphans approached Harriet shyly. She reached down and took the girl's hand.

"Absolutely. Come on, husband, it's time to cut the cake."

For the the first word about new releases, sales, and special notices, sign up for Charley's newsletter. https://charleymarsh books.com/mystery-newsletter/

ABOUT THE AUTHOR

In her younger days Charley Marsh's curiosity drove her to climb mountains, canoe rivers, and explore caves and wilderness areas from Maine to California. She's been shot at, caught in a desert flash flood, and almost drowned off the Maine coast. Once she tobogganed down a 5,000+ foot mountain.

Life is always an adventure if you have the right attitude.

Charley never set out to be a storyteller, but looking back on the elaborate lies she made up as a troubled teen she can see that she always had the makings.

If you would like a full list of Charley's books or simply want to contact Charley visit: https://charleymarshbooks.com/